FULL CIRCLE

D Foster showed up a few months before Tupac got shot that
first time and left us the summer before he died. By the time
her mama came and got her and she took one last walk out
of our lives, I felt like we'd grown up and grown old and lived
a hundred lives in those few years that we knew her. But we
hadn't really. We'd just gone from being eleven to being thirteen. Three girls. Three the Hard Way. In the end, it was just
me and Neeka again.

ALSO BY JACQUELINE WOODSON

After Tupac and D Foster

JACQUELINE WOODSON

After Tupac and D Foster

PUFFIN BOOKS
An Imprint of Penguin Group (USA)

PUFFIN BOOKS
Published by the Penguin Group
Penguin Group (USA) LLC
375 Hudson Street
New York, New York 10014

USA ★ Canada ★ UK ★ Ireland ★ Australia
New Zealand ★ India ★ South Africa ★ China

penguin.com
A Penguin Random House Company

First published in the United States of America by G. P. Putnam's Sons,
a division of Penguin Young Readers Group, 2008
Published by Puffin Books, a division of Penguin Young Readers Group, 2010

THE LIBRARY OF CONGRESS HAS CATALOGED THE G. P. PUTNAM'S SONS EDITION AS FOLLOWS:
Woodson, Jacqueline.
After Tupac and D Foster / Jacqueline Woodson
p. cm.
Summary: In the New York City borough of Queens in 1996, three girls bond over
their shared love of Tupac Shakur's music, as together they try to make sense
of the unpredictable world in which they live.
ISBN: 978-0-399-24654-8 (hc)
[1. Coming of age—Fiction. 2. Friendship—Fiction. 3. Shakur, Tupac, 1971–1996—Fiction.
4. African-Americans—Fiction. 5. Queens (New York, N.Y.)—Fiction.]
I. Title
PZ7.W84945Af 2008
[Fic]—dc22 2007023725

Puffin Books ISBN 978-0-14-241399-9

Printed in the United States of America

15 17 19 20 18 16 14

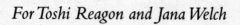

For Toshi Reagon and Jana Welch

The summer before D Foster's real mama came and took her away, Tupac wasn't dead yet. He'd been shot five times—two in the head, two down by his leg and thing and one shot that went in his hand and came out the other side and went through a vein or something. All the doctors were saying he should have died and were bringing other doctors up to his room to show everybody what a medical miracle he was. That's what they called him. A Medical Miracle. Like he wasn't even a real person. Like he was just something to be looked at and turned this way and that way and poked at. Like he wasn't Tupac.

D Foster showed up a few months before Tupac got shot that first time and left us the summer before he died. By the time her mama came and got her and she took one last walk on out of our lives, I felt like we'd grown up and grown old and lived a hundred lives in those few years that we knew her. But we hadn't really. We'd just gone from being eleven to being thirteen. Three girls. Three the Hard Way. In the end, it was just me and Neeka again.

The first time Tupac got shot, it was November 1994. Cold as anything everywhere in the city and me, Neeka, D and everybody else was shivering our behinds through the winter with nobody thinking Pac was gonna make it. Then, right after he had some surgery, he checked himself out of the hospital even though the doctors was trying to tell him he wasn't well enough to be doing that. That's when everybody around here started talking about what a true gangsta he was. At least that's what all the kids were thinking. The churchgoing people just kept saying he had God with him. Some of the parents were saying what they'd always been saying about him—that he was heading right to what he got because he was a bad example for kids, especially black kids like us. Crazy stuff about Tupac being a disgrace to the race and blah, blah, blah. The wannabe gangsta kids just kept saying Tupac was gonna get revenge on whoever did that to him.

But when I saw Tupac like that—coming out of the hospital, all skinny and small-looking in that wheelchair, big guards around him—I remember thinking, *He ain't gonna try to get revenge on nobody and he ain't trying to be a disgrace to anybody either. Just trying to keep on.* Even though he wasn't smiling, I knew he was just happy and confused about still being alive.

Went on like that all winter long, then February came and they sent Tupac to jail for some dumb stuff and people started talking about that—the negative peeps talking about that's where he needed to be and all the rest of us saying how messed up the law was when you didn't look and act like people thought you should.

Spring came and Pac dropped his album from prison and this one song on it was real tight, so we all just listened to it and talked about how bad-ass Pac was—that he wasn't even gonna let being in jail stop him from making his music. Me and Neeka and D had all turned twelve by then, but we still believed stuff—like that we'd grow up and marry beautiful rapper guys who'd buy us huge houses out in the country. We talked about how they'd be all crazy over us and if some other girl walked by who was fine or something, they wouldn't even turn their heads to look because they'd be so in love with us and all. Stupid stuff like that.

In jail, Pac started getting clear about thug life, saying it wasn't the right thing. He got all *righteous* about it and whatnot, and with all the rappers shooting on each other and stuff, it wasn't hard to agree with him.

Time kept passing on that way. Things and people chang-ing. First, D turned thirteen, then me and Neeka were right there behind her—us all turning into teenagers, getting body, getting tall, boys acting stupid over us.

Seems soon as we started settling into all that changing, D's mama came—took her away from us.

And time kept on creeping.

Then Tupac went and died and it got me thinking about D. About the short time she was with us and about how you could know somebody real good but not know them at the same time. And it made me want to remember. Yeah, I guess that's it. I guess that's what I'm trying to do now. . . .

PART ONE

Maybe, while he was in jail, Tupac started thinking about his Big Purpose. That's what D called it—our Big Purpose. She said everybody's got one and it's just that we gotta figure out what it is and then go have it.

The night she said it for the first time, it was late in the summer 1995 and we were all just hanging out—me, her and Neeka—watching music videos on TV. Before they started coming on regular, we'd have to watch the bootleg copies and sometimes those were so bad, we could hardly see the people in them. If it was a Tupac video, the only thing all the girls wanted to see real good was Tupac's eyes. He had the prettiest eyes of any rapper—they were all big and sad-looking and he had dark eyebrows that were so thick, they made you think about soft things.

That night, they showed "Brenda's Got A Baby," one of Tupac's old videos where Tupac sang about the young girl getting pregnant, and in the video Tupac was holding the baby because Brenda had put it in a garbage can. Me, Neeka and D was sitting on the floor in my living room. We'd put our money together and had enough for a small pizza and a liter of Pepsi. With a small pie, everybody could have at least two slices. D hadn't eaten anything since school lunch, so her eyes got real wide when she realized how much we had.

"Dag, my girls!" she said, her smile getting all big. "We gonna eat like we stupid tonight!"

And we did. We'd each had our two slices and were working on the last two, passing the slices back and forth between us—me taking a bite, then passing it to Neeka, Neeka taking a bite, then passing it on to D. D had the slice when Tupac's video came on.

"They don't hardly never be playing Pac," she said. "It's like they scared of him or something."

It was dark in the living room except for the blue light

coming off the screen. D got real quiet and stopped eating. I could see the shiny line of pizza grease moving past her bony wrist and on down her arm.

"Hey D," Neeka said. "You babysitting that slice? Pass it on, girl."

But D just kept staring at the TV like she couldn't hear anymore, holding the slice up, frozen in midair.

"Forget about it," I said. "I'm done anyway."

I leaned back against the couch. Tupac's beautiful eyes came up close on the screen. His mouth moved slowly as he sang about Brenda never ever really having a chance in life. His eyes looked sad like he was really singing about the truth and somebody he knew real good. Maybe he was thinking about his own mama—how she'd been in jail when she was pregnant with him. Not because she'd done something real wrong or anything—just because she was in this militant group, the Black Panthers. Back in the day, the Black Panthers were always marching and trying to get things changed so that black people could live a little bit better—like they're the reason there was free breakfast in school and stuff like that. Tupac's mama had gotten arrested and when she went to jail, she started making changes there—making sure pregnant women had decent food so that their babies could be born healthy and all. Everybody who knew Tupac knew about his mama. He loved her more than anything. Maybe Tupac was singing about Brenda but really thinking about his own mama—how she could have just thrown him away but she didn't. Instead, she made sure he was born healthy. And strong.

"Him and me," D said, real quiet. "It's like we the same in some crazy way."

Neeka looked at me and made a face.

"The only way you and him's the same," Neeka said, "is that you both Nee-groes. But you broke-ass and Tupac's got some money in his pockets."

D kept staring at the TV. Tupac was walking slow with his boys all around. His head down. He was so beautiful, I felt like I could see Brenda inside of him. Like even though he was singing about a girl who threw her baby away, he was thinking about himself. Made me wonder if he was seeing himself as Brenda or the baby.

"It's like I look at him and I see myself. It's like I'm looking in a mirror," D said. She turned to the pizza slice she was holding, like she was just remembering it was there, then reached past Neeka. "Here," she said, handing it to me. "I'm full."

"Me too," I said, pushing the slice back at her. She dropped it into the empty pizza box, then took a napkin and wiped the oil off her arm.

"You should just rub that in," Neeka said. "Your arm's all ashy."

"You hush!" D said. But she was smiling.

"You still ain't tell me what else you got in common with Tupac," Neeka said.

"Was your mama in jail like his mama?" I asked.

D shook her head. She curled her fingers into her palm and stared down at them.

"My mama is somewhere being somebody's hot mess."

She got quiet for a minute. "He sings about things that I'm living, you know. When he be singing the 'Dear Mama' song, that makes me think about my own mama. It's like his mama was a mess sometimes and he still loved her—people's moms be all complicated, and it's not like you got a bad mama or you got a good mama the way people be trying to judge and say."

D smiled.

"It's like he sees stuff, you know? And he *knows* stuff. And he be thinking stuff that only somebody who knows that kinda living deep and true could know and think."

"Yeah," Neeka said. "And he gets paid big dollars for those thoughts. That's way, way, *way* different from us."

The Tupac video went off and Public Enemy came on. I couldn't stand PE with their stupid big clocks around their necks and all that military stuff. It didn't make any sense to me.

Neeka and D didn't like them either. I turned the sound down.

"Y'all spending the night?" I asked.

Neeka nodded but D shook her head.

"Flo said she'd beat my behind if I didn't come home." She got up off the floor. Her foster mom's name wasn't Flo, we just called her that. Short for Foster Lady Orderly. It was real late for D to be taking the bus back to Flo's house. She started putting on her sandals and getting her stuff together. We'd been friends for almost a year but we'd never seen where she lived.

"We gonna walk you to the bus stop," I said, getting up off the couch. "C'mon, Neeka."

"You sure lucky," D said to Neeka.

"For what?" Neeka stretched real high and yawned, her skinny brown belly showing out from under her T-shirt.

"Just 'cause you get to spend the night." D took a brush out of her pocketbook and brushed her hair. It was straightened, but Flo wouldn't let her wear any styles except two cornrows or a whole lot of box braids. Whenever D got around our way, she took the cornrows out and just let her hair be free. But she always remembered to put it back like it was before she got on the bus.

"You should just tell the crazy lady you almost grown," Neeka said. "And then come around here and let me hook you up with some fly hair and some good fashion."

D stopped brushing. I clicked the TV off and turned on the light. We all squinted against the brightness.

"Dag, girl," Neeka said. "Give a sister a warning before you turn on a light."

"Why you always gotta say that, Neeka?" D was pointing the brush at her.

"Say what?"

"Tell me to go tell Flo about herself."

"'Cause you *should*."

"And then what?" D looked mad now. Her eyes were dark green—pretty in a strange way, like they should have been on somebody different but at the same time looking like they almost belonged to her. Her skin wasn't brown like mine or light brown like Neeka's—it was kinda *tan* brown in that way that made people always ask her what she was mixed with. When she said, "I'm half black and half your mama!" me and Neeka would laugh and the person would either get mad or laugh too. D hated people asking what she was. Maybe because she didn't know who her daddy was.

Neeka rolled her eyes. "If you told Flo to kiss your butt, she'd see you was half grown and stop treating you like somebody's baby."

"Last I heard, twelve wasn't half grown—"

"In six years, you'll be eighteen," Neeka said. "You eighteen, you legal."

"If I *make it* to eighteen. If I don't act right, I'm out of the system and on my own. And probably *homeless*. I been in the system long enough to see how jacked up it is. Kids living in the streets because they couldn't get along with their foster mamas. Kids all caught out there and whatnot. I am *so* not trying to go down like that." D put the brush in her bag and started braiding, her hands flying through her hair like she'd been braiding it for a hundred years.

"Why you getting so tight about it, D? Dag. I was just *saying*."

D finished the first braid and started on the other one. "You my girl, Neeka, but you got your folks looking out for you."

Neeka started to say something, but D put her hand up.

"Let me finish. You got that nice house and cute clothes and stuff. All I got right now is Flo, and if Flo says go, then I gotta go. I ain't ready to be trying to figure out how to fit in with some other family somewhere. I'm just trying to fit in with Flo."

"She just trying to go with the Flo," I said.

D looked at me and smiled.

"You corny," Neeka said.

D finished her other braid and looked at her watch—she'd bought it for ten dollars in Times Square, and most of the time it worked. She always wore it and was always checking it.

We headed out. It was warm outside. Some grown-ups were sitting on their stairs across the street next door to Neeka's house. We waved and they waved back. Neeka's mama, Miss Irene, must have smelled us leaving, because she raised her window.

"Neeka, where you all think you going this late?" she yelled across at us.

Neeka rolled her eyes and cursed softly. "That woman's got *radar*, yo!" she whispered. "We're just walking D to the bus stop, Ma! Then I'm gonna sleep over at—"

"Oh, now you're *telling* me what you're going to do?" Miss Irene said. She must have been in the middle of doing her hair because half of it was straightened, hanging down to her shoulder, and the other half was curling above her ear.

"Just go with the Flo," D whispered.

"Can I . . . ?"

"You call me when you get back inside and we'll talk about it," Miss Irene said. "You be safe going home, D."

"I will, Miss Irene," D said, and Miss Irene slid the window back down to meet the screen and disappeared into the house.

We knew she'd let Neeka stay. For some reason, moms felt like they had to put on acts and let you know who had all the power.

Neeka put her hands in her pockets and frowned all the way to the bus stop. But the minute we turned the corner, me and D started cracking up.

"She caught you out there, Neeka." D laughed.

"Can't creep around Miss Irene," I said. I did the creep-step from Michael Jackson's "Thriller" video.

"You lucky you don't have some real mama all up in your stuff," Neeka said to D.

We got to the bus stop and D took a deep breath. The avenue was quiet the way it usually was. Most times, the loudest sound was the bus pulling up. But for a while, there wasn't even that.

"One day, my mama's gonna show up again and things will all settle back to how they once was . . ."

Me and Neeka looked at each other. It wasn't the first time

D had mentioned her mama coming back. Me and Neeka had believed her in the beginning. But after a lot of time passed with no real mama coming, we stopped. We didn't tell D that. She was our girl and she needed to keep on keeping on like that.

"That's gonna be tight," D said softly. "Real tight."

"Yeah," Neeka said. "Until she puts you on lockdown worse than Flo."

"Or worse than *your* mama," D said, and me and her started cracking up again.

Neeka tried not to, but she couldn't help smiling.

"You remember how our mamas were when you first starting coming around?" Neeka said. "All suspicious and whatnot."

"Like you were going to ruin their innocent girls," I said. "Meanwhile, Neeka already looking at every boy that got half a leg and—"

"It wasn't deep," D said, cutting me off. A look came across her face, tired, old like a grown-up. "I would have been suspicious of me too—coming to this nice neighborhood out of nowhere. No mama or dad or even little sister to be coming over here with me."

"They got cool about it, though. My moms was just glad I had another friend," I said.

"And my moms was just glad you had some sense. And being how she seems to love kids so ding-dang much, she probably fell asleep dreaming me and you was a third set of twins in the family."

Me and Neeka laughed. D smiled, but she looked faraway. Like she was already on that bus and gone.

"I used to be roaming all over the place," D said. "And I'm glad because it got me here."

"Why *did* you roam, though?" I asked. Whenever D talked about her roaming, I always asked why. I wanted to under-stand—deep—what it was like to step outside.

D looked at me and shook her head. "Why? Why? Why, Miss Why? You know *why*."

"I know you be telling us why, but I still don't get it. You say you want to see how other people be living, but that still don't make a lot of sense to me."

"You really not curious about how other people be living?"

"Yeah right," Neeka said. "I guess you read all those biog-raphies and all them other books just to feel the pages turn-ing between your fingers."

"Shut up, Neeka. I'm talking to D. Doesn't have anything to do with the books I read."

"Yeah it does," D said quietly. She looked at me, her green eyes like tiny mouths asking me all these questions—*Don't you ever want to know the answers?* they were saying. *The real answers . . . to everything?*

"Uptown they got those fancy buildings. Out in

Brooklyn they got those pretty brownstone houses. West Side got Central Park and people going all over the place in those bright yellow taxicabs." D looked at us and I knew a part of her knew how much me and Neeka lived for the rare moments when she talked about her life, when she showed us where she'd been and, by doing so, we got to go to those places too.

And then it made sense to me—crazy-fast sense in a way it hadn't before. D walked out of her own life each time she stepped into one of those other places. She got off the bus or walked up out of the subway and her life disappeared, got replaced by that new place, those new strangers—like big pink erasers. Before me and Neeka started asking D about her life, we were erasers too—she got to step into our world, with all the trees and mamas calling from windows and kids playing on the block, and forget.

"I can't even imagine being as free as you," Neeka said. "I'd be all over the place!"

"That's why your mama got you on lockdown," I said.

"Like yours doesn't?" Neeka said back.

D laughed, but then she said, "Some days I be feeling like I'm *too* free."

"You really think there's such a thing as *too free*?"

"Heckio no!" Neeka said. "And I can tell you for a fact, D—you'd be kissing all that good-bye with a real mama."

D leaned her head on Neeka's shoulder and smiled. "I'm done, girl. That's what I'm saying. I seen everything I want to see. Lockdown like *that*? I'm ready. As long as it comes with my mama."

D started singing real soft "Dear Mama," the Tupac song where he talked about having a beef with his moms but loving her anyway. D knew all the words and she moved real sweet when she did the rap parts. But when the chorus came on, she just stayed still and sung it—*I love you. I need you. I appreciate you*—over and over until the song was done.

We got quiet. An ambulance raced by, and way down the avenue, somebody started honking their car horn like they didn't have any sense. It was June now and school was out for the summer. Our neighborhood was usually quiet even in the summertime. It had always been like that, boring and quiet with some kids and some teenagers and a whole lot of parents up in all of our business. It was the kinda block where somebody was calling your mama if you even talked too loud. Crazy how grown people liked their quiet.

We loved D because she was our girl and because she'd been to places and seen things me and Neeka probably weren't ever gonna see. Even though Flo had her on lockdown at night, D also had all this freedom in the daytime. I leaned against the bus stop sign and watched her and Neeka. Mostly I was the quiet one in our group, the Brain. Mostly I watched and listened. But I could watch until I was ninety-nine and I'd never be able to see what D saw.

"The way I figure it," D said, "we all just out in the world trying to figure out our Big Purpose."

"Oh, now you gonna go get all *relevant*," Neeka said. *Relevant* was one of her favorite words. A lot of rappers used it and Neeka used it whenever she could too. "Well, drop your knowledge."

"I'm serious, Neeka. My Big Purpose ain't about telling Flo to let me do whatever I want to do. I could do that and then be out on the street tomorrow. And the street is *not* my Big Purpose."

"What's your purpose, then," I asked. "I mean, what's your *Big* Purpose?"

D smiled.

"You my girls," D said. "You been my girls for a long time now and we tight like it's all right. Everybody knows that. Everybody see us coming say, 'Here come—'"

"Three the Hard Way," we all said.

"I know I got this Big Purpose. And when I know what it is exactly, I'm coming right to y'all with the news."

The bus came and D kissed me and Neeka good-bye and climbed on. We watched her pay her fare, walk to the back and climb into a window seat. There were only a few other people on the bus and D pressed her forehead against the window and gave us the power peace sign. Me and Neeka gave it right back to her and stood there until the bus pulled away. She kept waving at us until the bus was way down the avenue.

Then me and Neeka headed back to our block. We'd lived across from each other since we was babies. If Neeka wasn't spending the night, she'd cross to her green house with the dark green shutters. Inside, Miss Irene would be fussing at the kids to be quieter and fussing at Neeka to help her get dinner ready before her daddy got home.

My house was painted white and had dark red shutters at the windows. Mama worked most days, so a lot of the time it was just me, myself and I. Some days, I'd just lay back on my bed and stare up at my ceiling. I'd stuck these glow-in-the-dark stars up there and some days I'd just stare at them until the light faded enough to see them real clear.

"You better call your mama the minute we get back," I said to Neeka.

"Why? She's probably still in the window clocking me."

"Just call, Neek."

Neeka nodded. Then we both got quiet. And stayed like that for the whole walk home.

CHAPTER TWO

Seems I'd always known Neeka. From our first baby steps, I remember the big hands of our mamas lifting us up out of the playpen. I remember the smell of our mamas' coffee and the way their voices got all quiet when they were gossiping while me and Neeka chased each other around their legs and laughed at stupid stuff, like Elmo and the way dust turned all shiny when it got in front of some sun.

Neeka had come running to me first when she kissed Tony Anderson in her hallway. "His lips tasted funny," she'd said, scrunching up her face. "Like old cigarette ashes or something." And later on, when we'd seen Tony up at the park, him and his boys passing a cigarette around, Neeka had run back home and started rinsing her mouth out real hard with mouthwash and a washcloth.

"How come you let me kiss that nasty old boy," she'd said. And I just sat there on her toilet seat, laughing at her craziness.

But D was different. She just appeared one day. Summer wasn't even over yet but fall was already turning a few of the leaves on our block red and gold. Me and Neeka had bought matching jean jackets with white stitching on the pockets for when school started and we'd worn them that day with these brown velvet pants we had. We'd walk up and down the block thinking we were bad, but we were just hot in our fall gear. We'd come back and sat down, hot and sweaty, on Neeka's stoop. Down from my house, some little kids were taking turns on a Sit 'N Spin toy and we watched them, one by one, get up off of it and fall down on the ground from dizziness.

When I looked away from watching them, I saw her standing across the street, leaning against somebody's gate, watching us. Something about the way she stood there, just looking— no smile, no frown, nothing—it just caught something in me. Made my heart jump a bit. Something about the way she stood there was real familiar to me, like the way I'd want to stand someplace new and watch people I didn't know.

"Who's that girl over there, staring us down like that?" I said to Neeka.

Neeka looked to where D was standing and shrugged. Then she stood up.

"You looking for somebody?" Neeka said. It wasn't a *real* unfriendly voice, just a little.

"Not really."

And I guess she thought that was an invitation to cross the street, because that's when she came over to us. I looked her up and down. She was tall and skinny and looked like she thought she was cute with her green eyes and pretty sort of half way of smiling at us. Her hair was in a bunch of braids with black rubber bands at the end of every single one. The braids were long, coming down over her shoulders and across her back, and her hair was this strange dark coppery color I'd never seen on a black girl—not *naturally*. She was wearing a T-shirt that said "HELLO MY NAME IS" in green letters, only there wasn't a name after that, so it didn't make any sense whatsoever. I looked down at her feet. She had on white-girl clogs like you saw on the girls on TV—the ones with blond hair who lived in places like California and Miami or somewhere. Everything about her was screaming *I'm not from around this way.*

"Those your real eyes?" Neeka asked, right off. I'd never

seen green eyes up close like that, but that wouldn't have been *my* first question.

"Yeah," D said. "Everybody be asking me that. This is my own hair too. Color and everything. It used to be real light but it's getting darker every year. Figure by the time I'm grown, it'll be jet-black."

I stared at her. Wondering what it would be like to have hair that changed like that, to have eyes that green against that tannish skin. She looked back at me and for a minute, or maybe for a few minutes, we just stared—like we were trying to take in every single bit of each other—each of us trying to figure the other one out.

"Y'all sisters?"

"Yeah," Neeka said. "We came from different mamas and different daddies, but we're sisters." She held up her hand and I slapped it, saying *You know it.*

"You always dress the same?"

Neeka shrugged. "You got a lot of questions for a stranger."

"You could ask me some questions too," D said.

"What's up with the shoes?" I said.

She looked down at her shoes, then back at me. Something changed in her face that made me sorry I'd asked.

"They just shoes," she said, looking off down our street. "I roam and they get me where I'm going."

Neeka looked at her, then leaned back and put her elbows

on the stair above the one she was sitting on. "What's your name?"

"I go by D," she said. "I don't have no sisters, that's why I'm asking about y'all."

"Well, I'm Neeka."

I told D my name and she sat down, a few steps below me and Neeka.

"I guess I'm kinda like an only child."

I frowned. "Like? Either you're an only child or you're not. There's no gray area." I watched her for a minute to see if she understood about gray areas. I'd just learned it myself and was trying it out.

"There's gray," she said. "If you don't really know, right? If you have some idea but ain't really sure." D looked right at me again. I knew I liked her then, even if she *did* wear white-girl shoes. Mama was always saying I was a brain snob, that I didn't like people who didn't think. I didn't know if that was *snobby*. Who wanted to walk around explaining everything to people all the time?

"But you the only kid in your house?" Neeka asked.

D nodded. "Yeah. Gets boring. So I roam." She looked off down the street again. "This is a nice block."

"Dag, you lucky," Neeka said. "I got about seventeen brothers and sisters. All running me crazy."

"She's got four brothers and two sisters," I told D.

"Yeah," Neeka said. "But you gotta count all the twins twice because they're bad. By the way," Neeka said to D. "Where *is* your house?"

D kept looking out over the block. "Around the way. Gotta take a bus from here."

"Well, what made you take the bus from *your* house over there in some vague place you don't seem to want to reveal to us," Neeka said, speaking slowly—like English wasn't D's first language or something. "To *our* street on *this* day and at *this* time?"

D smiled. I didn't know then that it was her real smile, the way her lips only turned up a little bit, the way her eyes got sort of sad. I didn't know that smile was gonna stay with me long after D had roamed on back out of our lives.

"I saw the trees," D said.

"The trees, huh?" Neeka was making a slow circle with her pointer down by her leg—the down-low cuckoo sign.

"Yeah," D said. "I saw all the trees and got off the bus and just starting roaming over this way. That's how I found y'all. So here I am."

"Yeah," Neeka said. "Here you are. How old are you anyway?"

"Be twelve at the beginning of October."

I stared at D. She looked older than me and Neeka because she was a little bit taller and already had some body going on.

"But it's only August, so you're eleven like us," Neeka said. "We're gonna be twelve next May. And you get to take the bus and the train by yourself? And 'roam' all over the place?"

"Sho' thang," she said, and it took me a minute to realize

she was saying *Sure thing*—saying it like the rappers be saying it. "Who's gonna be taking them with me?"

"Dag! How long you been taking the bus by yourself?" Neeka asked, trying not to sound too jealous.

"Forever and a day," D said.

Neeka gave me a look. We weren't allowed to go *anywhere* by ourselves.

"Flo works," D said.

"Flo your mama?"

D nodded. "Kinda." She stood up and brushed off her pants.

Neeka rolled her eyes. "You got a lot of kind-ofs up in your vocabulary. You *kind of* vague."

D shrugged. "Yeah." She looked up at the sky. "All I know is I been roaming all day. Figure I better get my behind home. Y'all want to walk me to the bus stop?"

"Nah," Neeka said, trying to sound bored. "I'm comfortable here."

"Me too," I said. "Plus, we're not really allowed to leave the block without permission."

D swung some of her braids over her shoulder. "Yeah, I met a lot of kids who can't go nowhere. Their mamas be strict like that."

"You know a lot of other kids?" I asked her.

D shrugged. "Not really . . ."

"Here we go again with the vagueness," Neeka said.

"Nah, I'm for real," D said. "I *meet* a lot of kids, but I don't *know* a lot of kids. Either they act shady or their mamas act shady, you know."

"People just stupid sometimes," Neeka said. "Be thinking they know stuff and they don't."

D nodded and her and Neeka smiled at each other. I almost felt jealous, but then I didn't. Neeka's brother Tash was a queen and people used to always try to talk junk about him around us. When we were little kids, me and Neeka would get into fights over it, but we finally just started ignoring and making believe it didn't hurt us deep to hear people hating on Tash. I figured that's what Neeka was talking about and if it was like a bonding thing, then we could all bond on it, because Tash was just as much *my* brother as he was Neeka's.

I looked down at my boots—they were new, dark green with black laces and thick soles that made me a little bit taller. But they were heavy and my feet were sweating and itchy.

When I looked up, D was watching me. She'd tucked one of her feet behind her leg like she was trying to hide her white-girl clogs. "I guess I should get going. I'll probably come back around this way, though."

"The trees'll be waiting for you," Neeka said. Then she smiled. "You got a rope?"

"Yeah."

"Well, next time you come," Neeka said, "bring it, all right?"

D nodded then and smiled, that same smile—but this time,

her whole face relaxed and it was one of the prettiest smiles I'd ever seen in my life.

"I'm cool with that," D said.

Me and Neeka watched D walk down the block and turn the corner.

"She seems cool," Neeka said.

I shrugged, staring at the corner long after D had disappeared around it. A part of me was still with her—turning that corner and heading off the block—on my own. Free like that.

And a few days later, when D showed up, she was wearing new sneakers and carrying the rope in her knapsack. As we stood there, unraveling it, talking about who'd be first and what rhymes we knew, D got real quiet.

"Feels like forever since I had me some friends to jump double Dutch with."

"Wherever Flo living is the wrong place to be," Neeka said. "'Cause around here, if you got a rope, you're *gonna* have some peeps to jump with."

"That's what it feels like," D said. "Feels real good coming back here."

"Long as you bring the rope," Neeka said.

"Oh, it's like that?" D said, playing along with Neeka's craziness.

"You know it is, girlfriend," Neeka said. "You know you gotta come to the table with something if you wanna eat."

"You can come even if you don't have no rope," I said. "Neeka's just messing with you. Repeating something she probably heard her mama saying."

"Don't talk about my mama," Neeka said.

"Ain't talking about your mama. I'm talking about *you*. That's why Jayjones be calling her a parrot."

"Who's Jayjones?" D wanted to know.

"Nobody," Neeka said. "A big nobody."

"A big fine nobody," I said. "He's Neeka's big brother."

A group of little girls came over and stood near us, watching us untangle the rope.

"Y'all doing double Dutch?" one of them asked.

"Yeah," Neeka said. "You can watch, but don't even be thinking about asking for a jump."

The little girls all nodded and it made me remember being little like that, watching the big girls jump.

"I don't mind going last," D said. She took the open end of the rope.

"I don't mind going first," Neeka said.

I picked up the closed end and me and D started turning.

"Slow down, y'all. It ain't a double Dutch *race*," Neeka said, and we slowed the ropes a little bit. When Neeka jumped in, we started counting.

"Ten, twenty, thirty, forty, fifty . . ."

And the three of us had a rhythm going.

CHAPTER THREE

Neeka's big brother Jayjones was going to be a pro ball player when he grew up. But in the meantime, he played ball for Grady High School and worked at KFC. At night he smelled like chicken grease and sweat, but he was so fine, most girls ignored the smell.

His full name was Jackson Jones, but the first time he got on a basketball team, he was just a little kid playing for the Police Athletic League.

There was another kid named Jones on the team, so they put J.JONES on one jersey and P.JONES on the other. After that, we all started calling him Jayjones.

When he was a freshman at Grady, he scored forty points in his play-off game and me and Neeka made T-shirts that said I KNOW J.JONES and wore them for a week straight. That felt like a long time ago. He was still a high scorer, but we weren't trying to wear any T-shirts about it anymore.

"Y'all want some chicken?" Jayjones asked, coming over to my stairs and sitting down with me, Neeka and D. It was Saturday and D had turned twelve the Monday before. Leaves were falling off the trees all over the block and even though it was October and we still had some warm days, most days you could tell winter was starting to get its groove on. But it was Saturday and the temperature had gone up to eighty degrees. We were all sitting on my stairs, trying to catch the last few crazy hot days. Jayjones was wearing his basketball shorts and his hair was braided in zigzag cornrows. His legs were long and skinny with big calf muscles. He had a dimple right at the top of his cheek and when he smiled, it got deep—making you do a double take if you didn't know him, because that was a strange place for a dimple to be. I saw D look at it. Then frown a little bit and look again. In the little while we'd known her, she'd met Jayjones a couple of times. I couldn't tell if she thought he was fine or not because she didn't say anything one way or the other about him. But I *knew* Jayjones thought D was cute. She'd only turned twelve, but she looked a lot older and guys were always trying to talk to her. Jayjones was see-through like all the others—you could look dead in their faces and see everything they were thinking about somebody.

Jayjones stretched his legs out down the stairs and crossed his ankles, his big basketball shoes looking a mile long. He held out the chicken box and Neeka took an extra crispy wing. D took a leg.

"Pretty girl like you should be eating a wing," Jayjones said, smiling at D to show off that dimple. D didn't say anything and Neeka told him to shut up.

"Like a wing's that different from a leg, fool," Neeka said.

Jayjones ignored her and held the box out to me. I waited for him to tell me to take a wing too, but he didn't. I shook my head and pushed the box back at him. It was too hot to be eating fried food anyway.

We had been talking about our families. D hadn't said much about hers, but Neeka was talking enough for both of them. She'd just finished giving D the four-one-one on her oldest brother, Tash, who was doing time for something stupid. Tash had gotten arrested right after D started coming around, so D hadn't got to know him like we did. Before Tash went to jail, he mostly hung out at the Piers in Greenwich Village where all the gay people seemed to hang out. Tash had been a sissy from day one and most people just accepted it. Sometimes when the rappers started going on and on about how much they hated homos, me and Neeka would turn the TV off. We didn't really talk about why—just both of us knew that crap was hard on the ear when the homos they were hating on was your own family.

Neeka was telling D how she came a few years after Jay-jones.

"And then," Neeka said, as if Jayjones hadn't even come over and interrupted us. "After she and my dad had Albert and Emmett, they had to go and have *another* set of twins. Had the nerve to have girl twins at that. *Crazy!* How you gonna have all those twins up in one family?" She rolled her eyes and took a bite out of her chicken wing. "So now we got"—Neeka started counting off on the hand that wasn't holding the chicken wing—"Tash, Jayjones, me . . ."

"Mama and Pops just like kids," Jayjones said, grinning. "When I go pro, I'm gonna buy them—"

"*If* you go pro," Neeka said.

"*When* I go pro," Jayjones continued, speaking over her. "I'm buying them a huge house like all the ballplayers be buying their mamas."

Neeka made a face. "Gonna have to be a big-assed house to get all of us up in it."

"It's gonna be a ONE-bedroom on a lake. The rest of y'all sorry behinds gonna stay right across the street. Hire a nanny for you."

Me and D laughed, but Neeka just rolled her eyes and took another bite out of her chicken. She'd blown her hair out and curled it. But the heat had started melting the curls, making them fall into her eyes and down her back. I brushed it back with my hand and Neeka smiled, grateful. So I got behind her and started finger-combing her hair back. It was jet-black and soft as anything. I tamed it into a braid.

"I owe you one," Neeka said.

"What kind of name is Albert anyway," I said. "No black people be naming their kids that. No white people either, for that matter. Your mama just run out of names?"

Neeka continued working on her chicken. "She named him that because she said he was born looking smart, like Albert Einstein, fool. You know that."

"Albert E wasn't smart," I said. "I read somewhere that he had some kind of brain disorder. Made him say all these crazy things that made sense to people a whole lot of years later. He had a *psychosis*."

Neeka looked at me. "Did you have to drink something to get that dumb? Because the good news is, eventually you'll pee it out."

"It's true," I said. "You deconstruct some of—"

"Uh-oh," Jayjones said. "Here she comes with the college words."

"You *take it apart*," I said. "Break the brother's language down. He wasn't saying nothing we didn't already know. He just had a way of saying it that made people feel confused and when peeps get confused, they have to figure out what to do. So they made him a genius. If you're a genius, it just means you confused some people somewhere."

"Okay, *genius*," Neeka said.

"Nah," Jayjones said. "She's smart." He winked at me. "That's cool. Colleges gonna be all over you."

"That's 'cause from the womb that girl been reading and stuff. Hiding behind those books," Neeka said. "I was reading *Cat in the Hat* and she was busting out some of those books ain't even have pictures in them."

I smiled—embarrassed. We'd had this conversation forever. Teachers, people on the block, Mama, Neeka—everybody was always talking about me being smart, how I'd leave them and go away to some fancy college. And maybe I would and maybe I wouldn't. I read all those books and watched those educational shows and peeped the newspapers and people's biographies and autobiographies because I was trying to see some tiny bit of myself up in those books. And even though I didn't ever find it, I kept on looking.

"See how she gets all quiet when we start calling her out," Neeka said. She turned and hugged me. "You know we just messing with you, girl."

"I know." But a part of me really didn't. Lately, I'd been feeling like I was standing outside watching everything and everybody. Wishing I could take the part of me that was over there and the part of me that was over here and push them together—make myself into one whole person like everybody else.

"Hey girl." Neeka tapped my knee. "Earth calling you home."

I swatted her hand away.

D looked at me and smiled. And I saw it then—the little part inside of her that was just like me, that was walking through this world trying to find the other half of her. She roamed the streets. I roamed the books. I smiled back. For some reason, in that split second, I knew no matter what happened, we'd always be connected.

Then Jayjones moved a little bit closer to her and D moved a little bit farther away. I tried to ignore that sickly feeling I got when he started acting all stupid around girls he liked.

"I shot four hundred free throws in the park last night," he said.

"How many went in?" D wanted to know.

Jayjones smiled, his teeth all straight and white. "Three hundred ninety seven."

"Well, what happened to the other three?" I said, wanting him to take his eyes off of D.

"Streetlight blew out." Jayjones looked at me and winked again.

I winked back. Jayjones was like a brother to me—a brother who I loved and was maybe a little bit in love with. But I knew D was pretty and it stung me to sit there and watch him looking at her like she was something beautiful and looking at me like I was just some kid.

D got up, put her chicken bones in the garbage and brushed herself off.

"I need to be getting to my bus."

Jayjones jumped up. "I'm gonna walk you."

"Whatever," D said, sounding bored.

Me and Neeka watched them walk down the block and turn the corner.

I watched Jayjones bump D's shoulder. Watched her bump his shoulder back.

The sun was starting to set, and down the block, somebody's mama was telling them it was time to come on upstairs. I hated that part of me that wanted D to turn that corner and disappear forever.

CHAPTER FOUR

So tell me about this D, Mama had said when D first started coming around. Across the street, Miss Irene was asking Neeka the same thing.

She's cool, Mama, me and Neeka answered in our separate houses.

Cool. What kind of cool? Get y'all in trouble cool? Drop out of school cool?

She gets A's and everything. Girl ain't even thinking about dropping out of school.

She the one got you saying "ain't"?

All through that fall, while Tupac's trial went on, while he sat in that courtroom and listened to that judge tell him why he was no good, while that girl changed and changed her story until all the judge had to go on was the fact that Tupac hit her on her butt and had THUG LIFE written on his belly, we watched it and our mamas tried to watch *us* with D, tried to see what was coming . . .

How could they know what was coming? How could we?

While Mama asked questions about D, I stared down at my hands and tried to answer.

One night, we sat at our kitchen table with her across from me—the tiny lines between her eyes getting deep with the wanting to know. To understand.

"She came out of nowhere and now the three of y'all thick as thieves."

"She lives around the way, Ma. That's *somewhere*."

"Well, who's her mama?"

"I don't know."

"Who's her daddy?"

"I don't know. She doesn't know either, I don't think. Her foster mom's probably home asking her the same question about *me*."

I stared out the window. Outside, snow was beginning to come down. It was the first snow of the year and the tiny white flakes made me think about being a little girl—me and Neeka all excited and stupid over the idea of playing outside. Sitting at the kitchen table with Mama, that cold gray winter-light coming in from outside making everything, even the toaster, look like it was on the verge of tears, it was hard to even believe there was a time when I got so happy and silly over something like snow.

"You know who your daddy is," Mama said.

I kept staring out at the snow.

"But I don't know *where* he is."

"Well, that makes two of us, baby. That sure makes two of us."

Mama got up from the table and went over to the sink. She wasn't heavy, but she wasn't skinny either. She'd had me when she was twenty and always said that she'd been real skinny before I was born. Where I was brown, Mama was light-skinned. Where my hair was thick and kinky, Mama's was thick and curly. Where I was tall, Mama was short—stopping just at my eyebrow. It seemed one day I was her baby, the next I'd gotten taller than her. Everything about me, Mama used to say, belonged to my daddy.

"I know you think about him," Mama said. "And I know you stick your head in all those books to disappear some days. I wish I could tell you exactly where he was, give you a phone number, even dial the phone for you."

I sat there, listening to Mama but staring out the window. She'd spent the whole morning asking me questions about D. I wanted to say, *Mama, there's always stuff we're not ever gonna know.* But I couldn't.

Mama always said about her and Daddy that staying together wouldn't have been good for anybody. But some days she sat by the window in the living room, just staring out over the block and looking sadder than anything. Those days I knew she was thinking of a better life, a different life. Something that maybe she'd planned for herself when she was my age. I thought back to me and Neeka and D jumping rope for the first time—how it felt like D had always been a part of me somehow. I thought about how we all three sat on the stairs on warm days, leaning up on each other and talking about all the stuff we were gonna do when we were grown and not broke anymore. I bit my lip. How could I explain even a little bit of this to Mama—how some days D smiled at me and felt like my missing half. She was not trying to judge me and Neeka for not being allowed to go off the block, not trying to get all up in my business about why I didn't have a daddy, not trying to be anything but D.

D was *home* to me and Neeka. D was *Ask me no questions and I'll tell you no lies.* She was *sun* and *crazy loud laughter* and *warm rain.*

After a few minutes, Mama said, "I just want you to

be careful. This D might seem nice, but who knows what she's gonna lead y'all into."

Who's her mama? Who's her daddy? Where's my daddy? Always stuff we ain't gonna know.

Outside, the snow fell all quiet. Outside, the world just kept going on and on.

Friday before Thanksgiving, we were on our block trying to teach some little girls how to jump. It was close to dinnertime and me, Neeka and D had gotten together right after school just to hang and jump some double Dutch. We'd been jumping for a while when the little girls came over and asked if they could play. We stopped jumping and let them use our rope. But after watching them try, we offered to help. They weren't even getting the basics of jumping in on one foot, though. Me, Neeka and D took turns jumping into the rope to show them how, but after a lot of time passed with them messing up, we gave up and went to sit on my stairs. It was cold out and we put pieces of cardboard under our butts to keep them warm. I had brought a comb, brush and some grease down so Neeka could braid my hair. She parted it down the middle, then starting brushing it.

"I guess that's why you just gotta learn yourself," D said, watching the little girls. "Can't nobody really teach you double Dutch."

"Nobody ever tried to teach us," Neeka said. "When I was little, the teenagers were like *'No!'* Remember?"

I nodded. "They were so not having us."

"Keep your head still," Neeka said, steadying my head with her hands. I felt the comb moving through it.

The girls had stopped trying to jump double Dutch and were doing single—two jumping while the other two turned the rope. They were doing "All in Together, Girls."

All, all, all in together, girls, how you like the weather, girls? Fine. Fine. Super fine. January, February, March . . .

You were supposed to jump out on the month of your birthday, but I guess since they didn't know how to jump in and out, they just kept going through all the months until they finally messed up.

Jayjones came running up the stoop all out of breath. He

sat down and put his head between his legs, taking some deep breaths before lifting it again.

"What's wrong with *you*, Jay?" Neeka asked.

Jayjones looked off down the block, then shook his head.

"Cops be trying to pull a brother down," he said. "I'm coming from the park just now, trying to get home, and this cop just *stops* me!" He pointed up the block. "Right up there on the corner and my house not even two minutes away! Talking about *What you running from, man?*" Jayjones took some more deep breaths. Even though it was cold out, there was sweat on his forehead and across his nose.

"I was like, *I ain't running from, I'm running to. Going home to see my family.* Some days I'm thinking why God gave me these legs to run if it's gonna mean getting stopped by some cop every time I try to do so."

Jayjones put his head between his legs again. I could hear him breathing real hard.

"That's why you need to stay your behind in school and figure out a way to get a job where you wear a suit every day," Neeka said. "Nobody be messing with a brother wearing a suit."

Jayjones raised his head and looked up the block again. He shivered, blew into his hands and sniffed.

"Brother in a suit is just a brother in a suit," he said. "His black head still sticking out the neck hole. And where you think I be going every day?"

"You cut class sometimes. I know that," Neeka said. She yanked the comb through my hair and I screamed. "Sorry, girl. You should have combed it out."

Jayjones gave her a look. "Then how come colleges are already writing to me? Asking me to think about coming?"

Neeka went back to combing. "'Cause you over six feet tall and can throw a ball in a basket, that's why. But they see those D's you be pulling down, they gonna say *never mind*."

Jayjones flicked his hand at her. "You're just being a parrot. Mama say it, then you say it. Mama say it again, then you say it again. Maybe when you grow up, you'll have a few thoughts of your own, little girl."

"You're gonna freeze your behind off out here," I said.

"My moms always tell him to put on a hat, but he act like he don't hear anybody," Neeka said. "Pneumonia ain't cute." She shivered and pulled her scarf tighter around her neck. "And why you running up on us like that, anyway? If I was a cop, I would've stopped you too."

"Where's your ball?" I asked him because he never walked down the street without it.

"Left it at school." He looked at Neeka. "Where I *was* today—for *all* my classes."

The little girls came over and gave us our rope back. They started to sit down on the stoop, but Neeka stopped them.

"Uh-uh," she said. "Shoo! You all don't need to be over here in grown folks' business."

"Grown folks?!" one of the girls said, putting her hands on her hips. "Y'all ain't grown."

"We growner than you," Neeka said.

The girl stuck her tongue out at Neeka and then she and the others ran down the block and around the corner.

Neeka stopped combing again. "They did *not* just leave this block," she said.

Jayjones threw his head back and laughed. Me and D smiled.

"Guess they are growner than you," Jayjones said. Neeka popped him with the comb.

CHAPTER SIX

One day I came home from school to find Mama sitting at the table reading about Tupac in the *Daily News.*

"This is a shame," she said, her hand wrapped around her coffee mug. "The only thing that boy's on trial for is so people can make some kind of example out of him."

I sat down across from her—reached for her

coffee and took a sip. It was bitter and sweet at the same time.

"No other evidence," Mama said. "But what that girl's saying he did and what's written on his stomach."

"Tell that to the people that be hating on him—saying he's a disgrace and all that junk," I said.

The picture in the paper showed Tupac with his shirt raised, showing off the tattoo on his belly: THUG LIFE.

Mama shook her head. "They say the judge didn't like the tattoo—didn't think it was something a person should write on themselves." Mama looked up at me. "That's that boy's own body. It's not the judge's business."

I stared at the newspaper for a long time. It was starting to seem like Tupac was actually going to do time.

"He ain't a thug," I said. "That's just his . . . his persona. The way he acts so people think he's a true gangsta."

Mama looked at me. "Wouldn't matter if he was," she said. "First Amendment says people got a right to freedom of expression without government interfering—everybody knows that. Judge doesn't like the way he looks, didn't like the way he is in the world, what he talks about, what's on his stomach . . . that's the crime here."

I nodded. Mama wasn't a big Tupac fan, but she was a big fan of justice.

"Guess that's why they're called judges," I said. "They get to judge people."

Mama shook her head, still looking down at the paper. "This world gets crazier and crazier," she said.

"You think the judge is really gonna make him do time, Ma?"

Mama rubbed her forehead with her palm, her eyes shut tight. When she opened them again, they were sadder than I'd seen them in a long time.

"Yeah, baby," Mama said softly.

That evening, the three of us—me, Neeka and D—sat on my stairs, until we were too cold to even shiver anymore. This *numbness* came over us, and we didn't even have to talk or curse or cry. Me, Neeka and D knew what we felt—way deep past all the cold. Past the coming darkness.

The next morning, me and Neeka walked into the kitchen already dressed for school to find Mama sitting with her head bowed toward the radio. There was a Tupac song playing and me and Neeka stopped dead in our tracks when the announcer came on and said the name of the song and told us Tupac had been shot five times the night before.

"They shot him?" Neeka whispered.

CHAPTER SEVEN

"News is saying somebody robbed him at some recording studio. Took forty thousand dollars' worth of jewelry from him and shot him up like that. I don't know what this world is coming to."

Mama put her hand over her mouth and shook her head real slow.

I sat down at the table, my body feeling heavy and old. Mama had made some bacon and eggs for us and the bacon was draining on a brown paper bag. I stared at the bacon—at the way the grease made dark stains on the paper—and felt some part of me get numb and still.

Neeka looked at me and her face didn't look familiar—it looked like it was falling all over itself to understand.

"They shot Pac?" she whispered again.

"Shhhh," I said because the newscaster was speaking again.

He said it was serious. He said one of the bullets landed somewhere near a lung. He said they were trying to stabilize Tupac. His voice went on and on.

Mama took a deep breath and got up. On her way over to the counter, she brushed her hand over my head. I grabbed her hand before she could pull it away, held it real tight and kept holding it as I let my head drop to the table, my tears like one long scream inside my throat.

"It's gonna be okay, y'all," Mama whispered. "It's gonna be okay."

I could hear Neeka crying. And someplace far away, I could have sworn I heard D's tears.

After school, D showed up, her eyes red and swollen, her hands cracked and cold from spending the morning roaming.

She took her coat off and sat on my couch rubbing the oil I'd given her into her hands.

"They hurt," she said. "I've walked through so much cold weather all my life and this is the first time my hands hurt like this." She put her head down on her lap and cried and then we all cried.

CHAPTER EIGHT

When we couldn't cry anymore, we took the boom box out onto my stairs.

Me and D was wearing our down coats and now D had gotten one somewhere but it looked old. We all had on gloves and hats and scarves and probably looked like crazy winter people. It was the first day of December and all over the block, people had started putting Christmas lights up on their windows. Across the street, in Neeka's house, the lights her father had put up blinked on and off—all green and blue and red and yellow. If you looked at them long enough, you'd probably lose your mind. I didn't know how Neeka lived in that house every year with those blinking lights. Ours were up too but they just stayed still.

The boom box was right next to us and every now and then D would try to flick it to a station with some news. With no sun shining, the wind picked up and had us shivering, but we didn't go inside. Something about the cold. It hurt like Tupac was probably hurting.

Jayjones came running up to us just as the sun was going down. He was out of breath by the time he got to the stoop, tiny puffs of cold air coming fast out of his mouth.

"Y'all hear about Pac?" Jayjones said, still catching his breath.

We all nodded and D pointed to the radio. "Been trying to keep up with the four-one-one all day long."

"They were trying to rob him," Jayjones said. "Sounds like a setup."

"You hear anything else?" I asked.

Jayjones shook his head.

"He's gonna be all right," D said, her voice real calm.

"Hope so," Jayjones said. He was wearing a heavy brown jacket with leather letters on it and some baggy jeans but no gloves or hat or anything. He blew into his hands and sat down across from D on the stair. After a moment, he said *It's crazy* so softly, you could barely hear it.

He leaned forward, his elbows on his knees. "I can't even imagine Pac being dead. How come it's like that? How come I don't even know him and he be feeling like a brother to me?"

He wasn't talking to us. Wasn't really talking to anybody. It's like we could have all disappeared and Jayjones would've just kept on talking.

"First time I heard Tupac, I was real young and he was with Digital Underground—dancing and getting a few lyrics in and whatnot. Even back in the day, it was like, Yo! He's gonna blow up."

"And then he was in that movie," I said. "Where he acted all crazy."

"*Juice,*" D said.

"Saw the bootleg," Neeka said. "Tash brought it home and we all watched it."

Jayjones looked at her and smiled. "I remember that."

"Yeah," D said. "But even before that—when he dropped his first album and that song 'If My Homie Calls'—that was the *It* right there."

"All through high school, girls by the dozens, sayin we cousins . . ." Jayjones sang.

"I'm down for y'all, when my homies call," D sang. "I was just a shorty," she said. "But that song, to me, it was all about having good friends." She looked at me and Neeka and, for the first time that day, she smiled. "I was doing all that moving around and I didn't ever think I'd have some homies like y'all be calling *me*."

"It was like he'd taken the crap I'd been going through," Jayjones said, "and spun it into this . . . these lyrics that just broke it all down. You know, he . . ." Jayjones looked at me.

"Clarified it," I said.

"Yeah," Jayjones continued. "He *clarified* it. And here I was, this kid up here in Queens trying to shoot a few baskets and get through the day—brother ain't know me from a can of paint."

D nodded.

Jayjones turned to Neeka. "You walk off this block and there ain't love like it is on these stairs. Brothers on the court be saying things about Tash make you want to holler. Tupac comes on and starts blasting them in the face about the hating and they can't do nothing but shut the hell up. 'Cause he's regular but he ain't regular. Gets big respect from people."

"Keep it real now, Jayjones," Neeka said, rolling her eyes. "Pac's lyrics ain't always cute when it comes to people like Tash. And anyway, tell me about what these chumps on the court be saying about my brother?"

Tash was a true-blue sissy and wasn't afraid to let the world know it. *Look at me,* he always used to say. *I can walk in heels better than any of these real girls out here, so if somebody wants to holler about it, I ain't gonna deny.* Even though he didn't really wear heels, everything about him said Queen—from his whispery way of talking to his swishy walk to his beautifully shaped eyebrows.

Jayjones just shook his head. "See, you just a little girl. Don't know what's up in the world."

"What I do know is if I catch somebody talking junk, it ain't gonna be pretty for them. And I also know this shooting is probably some more of that gangsta nonsense," Neeka said.

"It's black," I said.

The wind had died down again and our street was so quiet now. The air felt so cold and everything seemed to just be waiting for the next thing.

"It's because we black and we kids and he's black and he's just a kid—even though he's twenty-three—and every single song he be singing is telling us a little bit more about what could happen to us and how the world don't really care ..."

"My mama *cares*," Neeka said.

I rolled my eyes. "I *know* your mama cares. Everybody's mama cares. It's not our mamas. It's the world. That place

59

you gonna go to when you leave this block! Like Jayjones is saying."

"Neeka ain't never leaving this block," Jayjones said. "She's gonna walk around the corner and come screaming back."

Neeka started to say something, but D cut her off with a look.

I wanted to tell Jayjones we could stay on these stairs for the rest of our lives, but we was already halfway gone. But Jayjones and everybody else would just look at me. Look at me like I was some crazy brainiac—who didn't know what I was talking about.

"When I listen to Tupac, " D said softly, "I be thinking about the way my life could've been, you know. Like he sings about being in his mama's belly when she was in jail and then when his mama started doing drugs and stuff and then when his mama's boyfriends was beating on him and all that crazy nonsense. Before I got to Flo's house, I'd seen all kinds of whacked stuff like that. I was at this one foster home and the lady would take the checks they sent her to buy us kids food and she'd be doing crack and stuff with it and we'd be sitting there hungry." She stared at her fingernails. Her right leg was jiggling. I wanted to put my hand on it, to stop it, to let that leg know everything was gonna be all right. "Some days I was so hungry, I couldn't even hardly move."

Neeka looked at me. I started to say something, but she put her finger to her lips. D never talked about her life and it was strange to hear her talking about it now.

"I don't care if I don't have cute clothes or if some days my hair be looking messed up—I just don't never want to be hungry like that again."

There were tears in her eyes but they weren't spilling down, just sitting there all shiny.

"I see Tupac rapping and I see he got that same look that I got—like we both know what it feels like to be that hungry, to want to eat something that bad. And then when you finally get something to eat, your stomach gets all cramped up around it and you can't even keep it *down*. Can't even keep it inside you."

"You know my mama ain't never gonna let you be hungry no more," Neeka said. "She ain't the best cook in the world, but there's always gonna be a plate for you."

"You my girls," D said back, her voice all choked up and hoarse.

I put my hand on D's head and slowly stroked her hair. After a few moments, she put her head down on her lap and started crying. Then we all just sat there, looking out over the street, crying quietly, for D, for Tupac, for our own selves.

"He ain't gonna die," D said.

"What makes you so sure?" Neeka asked. I wiped my eyes and took a deep breath.

"It ain't his time. I don't feel it."

"So you all psychic now."

"All day long I been thinking about it, you know." She looked at Neeka. Watch him come back stronger. Shot like

61

that—you either say 'I'm out' and you die, or you hold on real hard. And come back stronger.

"I know it sounds whack," she said, so softly it sounded like she was talking to herself almost. "But when I see him on TV, I be thinking about the way his life was all crazy. And my life is all crazy. And we both all sad about it and stuff. But we ain't trying to let the sad feelings get us down. We ain't trying to give up."

We all got real quiet. I wanted D to just keep on going but she didn't. She just sat there a few minutes, looking up at the streetlight. Then, without saying anything, she got up, waved without even looking at us and started heading down the block. After a minute passed, Jayjones jumped up and ran up to her. He put his arm around her shoulder—not like a boyfriend but like a big brother—the way he did sometimes with me and Neeka. D walked with her head down, her hands inside her coat pockets.

"May as well sleep over at your house again tonight," Neeka said, wiping the snow from her face and getting up. "So we can keep up with this craziness."

"Neeka," I said as we headed into my house. "You think we the lucky ones?"

Neeka stopped at the bottom stair leading up to my apartment. It was warm in our hallway. Someone had baked something sweet and the smell made me hungry.

"Like how?"

I shrugged. "I don't know. When I heard D talking about

her life like that . . . when she was saying about being hungry and—"

"If we so lucky, how come she's the one get to take the bus all over the city *by herself* and don't have to worry about being home until nine o'clock?"

I didn't say anything. I wondered where Tupac's mama was. Wondered if she'd heard any news.

CHAPTER NINE

Tupac got better and the judge sent him to prison. The morning the sentencing came down, it was Valentine's Day. I'd gotten Mama a small red heart filled with chocolate-covered cherries and she'd given me a box of peanut clusters—the kind with the nuts and caramel and chocolate working all together to taste crazy in your mouth. I'd only eaten one, but she hadn't eaten any of her candy yet. We just sat there, reading the articles over and over while the radio played Tupac songs. The news said Tupac had touched a girl on her behind and the judge said that since he was such a thug, he was gonna show him a lesson. Up to four and a half years. Maximum security. They'd sent him off to Rikers Island that morning. From there he'd go upstate.

That afternoon on TV, they showed Tupac leaving the courtroom. He walked slowly, with his head down. When he got outside, he lifted his eyes, and slowly his beautiful, sad eyes looked into the camera and out at the world. Then he lowered his head again and his whole body seemed to sag. His whole body seemed to say, *How did this happen to me?*

Then it seemed like all over Queens, brothers were getting arrested and sent upstate. It felt crazy to turn on the television and see rappers talking about prison and doing these video scenes in prison and then to turn around and see your own people getting sent away. It was all crazy real and feeling like some kind of strange dream at the same time—people we didn't even know singing and rapping our stories.

But I was still a few months away from twelve when I was first starting to understand. And I'd sit in my room watching the stars on my ceiling begin to fade up into a glow and I'd just try to figure it all out. Just a little kid really without any of the words I needed to explain all the things my mind was just beginning to think about.

In May, me and Neeka turned twelve and Jayjones treated

all of us to McDonald's—buying us whatever we wanted. *Just Big Macs, fries and shakes for all of us,* Neeka said. *And don't forget to hook us up with some of those pies that always be burning our mouths.* And when Jayjones came to the table with our food, we all sang the Stevie Wonder birthday song real loud.

PART
TWO

"Brothers be hunted," Jayjones said one Sunday morning. We were walking home from church. In front of us, Miss Irene and my mama each held one of the twin girl's hands and talked real soft about Tash and the fact that he'd just been transferred to another prison, right near the one he'd already been doing time in. It was cold out. The summer had flown past us and before we could even get used to all the warm weather and freedom, fall came. We got taller and D turned thirteen and by then Neeka's body had started catching up to D's. I was still tall and skinny, but some curves were starting to happen for me too. By November, we couldn't walk anywhere without boys hollering at us.

I wanted to tell Jayjones that sisters were hunted too—boys screaming behind you and whatnot. Trying to touch you when you walked past them like they had some kind of right to your body. It was *crazy*.

Neeka shivered. Maybe she was thinking the same thing.

November had come on quick and cold and the only good part about the whole fall was that Tupac had gotten out of jail and was making videos again.

Jayjones had his hands in the pockets of his Sunday coat. Neeka was on one side of him and I was on the other. Emmett turned around and stopped when he heard Jayjones, but Albert kept on walking.

"Like people hunt for deer, Jay?" Emmett said, his eyes getting wide.

"Worse than that," Jayjones said. He was frowning. He'd frowned all through the church service and even as we were leaving and all of us shook the pastor's hand.

"You gotta walk crazy slow and not be in the wrong place or be driving the wrong car—like a Jaguar or a Mercedes or something."

"I can't drive no nice car?" Emmett said. "What if I buy it with my own money?"

"Then you better drive it real slow."

Emmett shrugged, then turned around and went to catch up with Albert.

"You be filling that boy's head with a lot of junk," Neeka said. "I'm going to tell Mama—"

"Mama knows!" Jayjones said. "She got four boys and one of them already in jail. She just holding on tight to the rest of us."

Neeka made a face.

"You think Tash deserves to be in jail?" Jayjones asked her.

"No."

"You think Tupac deserved to be in jail?"

"Of course not."

"Then multiply that and then multiply what you get and keep on multiplying."

"I read they be building more jails than schools," I said.

Jayjones put his arm around my shoulder. It felt warm and nice there. He put his other arm around Neeka's. She made another face but let him keep it there.

"Keep reading," Jayjones said. "You gonna have more people than my thick-headed sister to be convincing about this stuff. It's crazy."

"Yeah," I said, moving a little closer in to Jayjones. "Real crazy."

CHAPTER ELEVEN

One Friday night that winter, me, Neeka and D were playing cards at my kitchen table when D said real soft, "Y'all want to roam with me?"

Me and Neeka looked at each other. Snow had fallen twice during the week and although the streets were plowed, it was still piled up against the curb and on the sides of our steps. Cars were still halfway covered from the plowing and the wind was kicking up like it was losing its mind.

"Where?" Neeka asked.

D shrugged. "We just go," she said.

Neeka's mom had said it was okay to spend the night over my house and D's curfew wasn't for another two hours. My moms was doing overtime, so I knew she wouldn't be home for a while.

"Off the block?" I said.

"No," Neeka said, rolling her eyes. "Let's just walk up and down the hallway stairs for about an hour." Then, even though we were the only ones home, she dropped her voice. "Yes, off the block! D gonna show us the world, girl!"

"So your mama and my mama could break our behinds?" I put down my cards and picked up the book I'd been reading about the Black Panthers. Back in the day, there'd been a revolution going on. "No, thanks." I leaned back and opened it to where I'd left off. "D's thirteen now—she's almost out of butt-beating times. But you and me straight up in them."

Neeka came over and snatched the book out of my hand.

"C'mon, Neeka. I'm reading about a *revolution*."

"Well, I'm talking about revolting so get dressed, girl, we gonna roam. My feet itching like I got athlete's foot."

"Your mama will knock you into next week," I said.

Neeka got on her coat, then went in the closet and threw mine to me. We both had down coats, brown with fur collars. D's coat was some kind of black wool with little pilly things all over it. She put it on and wrapped a bright green scarf around her neck, then put on the hat that matched it. With the scarf and the hat on, the coat didn't look that bad.

"Oh—we are *so* out of here," Neeka said, her grin getting all wide.

I pulled my coat on slowly. We'd been to Manhattan and out to Brooklyn with our mamas but always by car and never by ourselves. The *Don't Leave the Block* rule was like something God had burned into those Ten Commandment tablets for Moses. Serious.

"This is crazy," I said, already feeling my two selves separating from each other—one going over to the couch with my book, the other one roaming. "I'm not going real far, y'all. I'm telling you that right now."

D nodded. "I got a place—it ain't far and it's only the bus—you don't even have to get on the train."

Neeka looked real disappointed.

"We don't have any tokens or anything." I started to take off my coat.

"I got it covered," D said. "It'll be cool, for real." She looked at Neeka, whose face was still all bent with disappointment. "We can't be going all the way to Manhattan—I gotta be home too early and your moms wouldn't be having it."

"We could just go to like the first stop in Manhattan— get out and walk around for a minute just to say we did," Neeka said.

I still had my coat half on, half off. "You can go there by yourselves."

"Forget it," Neeka said. She gave me a look. "Let's just go wherever. Least we'll be getting off the block."

When we got outside, we took a quick look up at Neeka's window to make sure her moms wasn't watching, then ran to the corner and around it without stopping.

By the time we got to the bus stop, we were out of breath and laughing. D got three tokens from her pocketbook and gave one to me and one to Neeka. "I bought a whole bunch 'cause Flo hit me with a twenty. After school, they don't be letting you use your bus pass anymore. Bus drivers be clocking it all careful and whatnot."

We sat there shivering—from the cold and from knowing what would happen if we got busted—until the bus came. Then me and Neeka put our tokens in the slot like it was something we did every day and followed D. There were a few other peeps on the bus and it was nice and warm. I felt the scared leaving me.

Neeka moved to a window seat and I moved to one on the other side. In the darkness, we could see our own neighborhood disappearing and the houses getting bigger and bigger. Soon, there weren't even that many streetlights—just darkness and the yellow light coming from people's windows. Then the houses got farther apart and it was spooky the way there weren't any people on the street, no corner stores or stairs to sit on. Just big front yards with tiny yellow lights glowing a path up to people's doorways. I stared out the window and hugged myself, trying to imagine what it would be like to grow up with not a lot of people on your street. Nobody calling you out the window. Nobody catching you sneaking off the block. It felt strange. Lonely. The only sound was the motor of the bus, and for some reason, it made me miss my mama. I leaned my head against the cold window glass.

"This is like way out—going out by Long Island," Neeka said.

I must have looked nervous, because D said, "Don't worry—I ain't taking you to Long Island."

We all got quiet and just stared out the window. People got off and the bus got emptier and emptier.

It seemed a long time passed before D said, "This is our stop," and we followed her off the bus.

When we got out, it was dark and cold. Me and Neeka stayed real close to D as we walked. When we came to the entrance of a big park, D stopped and smiled. The moon had come out and there were a few lights but mostly it was dark.

"We're here," D said.

Neeka looked at her. "You *must* be high."

I didn't say anything. The cold air felt good—not wet and hard like it had felt earlier. The wind had stopped losing its mind and the snow looked like it was glowing where the moonlight hit it.

"C'mon," D said.

"You think I'm going into that dark park to get beat up and raped and who knows what all else peeps thinking about doing to little girls?" Neeka said.

"Oh," I said. "So now we 'little girls' again. Back at the house, you were all grown and ready to go."

"Not to nobody's dark park I wasn't."

"Neeka," D said. "It's winter. It's dark. It's cold. How many other people trying to be in a park on a night like this?"

"The crazy ones," Neeka said back. "And that's who's gonna come after us."

"Ain't no one up in this park but us—once we get in there," D said. She started walking. Neeka looked at me and I shrugged and followed D. After another minute passed, I heard Neeka curse and run to catch up to us.

We walked down a whole lot of stairs and across a field. Then we came to a big stage.

"It's called an amphitheater," D said.

"We gonna get our behinds whipped for some broke-down stage?" Neeka said.

I turned and realized the stairs we'd just walked down were actually seats carved into the stone. They were covered with snow and moss. Behind the highest ones on one side, there were a whole bunch of trees—like a half ring. The moon was shooting through those bare trees and making all these shadows and light on the stage. Everything about the amphitheater looked older than anything or anybody. I hugged myself and smiled. It was like this place had always been here and always would be. I kept walking toward the stage, slowly. I wanted to walk in that moonlight. I wanted it on my back and head and face. Everywhere.

"Where you going?" Neeka yelled, and her voice echoed back over us.

I turned and smiled. "It's crazy! *Stupid!*" I said. "D. It's . . . beautiful!"

D smiled. "That's why I brought my girls here."

The stage wasn't high but it was carved from the same stone as the seats. At the back of it was this huge stone wall that seemed to go on forever.

For a minute, all three of us just stood there staring. I shivered. Something strange happened. With all that beautiful stone around me and the moon shining through the trees and down on us like that . . . and us three just standing there staring up . . . I felt whole—like my two selves had come together—finally meeting for the first time. I closed my eyes and hugged myself harder. I wanted to hold on to this feeling. For always.

We climbed up on the stage and me and D threw our arms up and yelled our names. And our names echoed back over us—all shadowy and hushed. We did it again. Then again. Then Neeka did it and smiled.

"We're here!" D yelled. And *We're here* came slipping back over us.

And inside my head, I heard myself saying, *I'm here.*

The stage was covered with snow and D was the first to lie down in it and make an angel. Then me and Neeka did it, shouting the whole time, *We're here! (I'm here.) We're here! (I'm here.)*

And lying in that cold snow with that beautiful moon shining above us and our own names floating down over us—nobody could have told me that we wouldn't always be here. That it wouldn't be me and Neeka and D—for always.

We left D on the bus and got off at our stop—me and Neeka walking real quiet back to my house. When we got there, my moms wasn't home yet and we peeled off our wet clothes and took turns taking hot showers. I stood under the water, wondering what situation D would go home to—wondering if Flo would ask her questions about her wet clothes and shoes. As the water poured over me, I couldn't help smiling again about the three of us on that stage with all that light around us.

When we were all done showering, me and Neeka sat on my bed in our pajamas drinking hot chocolate. We didn't say anything for a long time, just grinned whenever we made eye contact.

Neeka took a last sip of hot chocolate, set her cup on my dresser, then lay back on my bed, her head wrapped in one of Mama's scarves to keep it from getting messy while she slept.

"I get it now," she said.

I nodded.

"D's cool. She's like from another planet. The Planet of the Free." Neeka sat up on one elbow and looked at me. "I'm gonna go to that planet one day."

I shook my head and laughed. "We did, girl! We went tonight!"

Neeka held out her hand and I slapped it. And we laughed like we were losing our minds.

The morning I turned thirteen, Mama came into my room and handed me a small box wrapped up in flowered paper. She kissed me on the cheek and stared at me for a long time.

"I can't believe I have a teenage daughter."

It was still early. All night long my legs had been hurting. Mama said those were growing pains, and somewhere during the winter, I'd gotten way taller than her and D and Neeka. It felt strange to walk around feeling like I was all arms and legs and body. I turned the box around in my hand wondering if there'd ever come a point in my life when I'd fit into my body. Maybe that's what was happening. Maybe the hurting was about those two selves—trying to come together—trying to fit into one body the way they had that night at the amphitheater. Only it hadn't hurt back then.

I opened the box slowly. Inside was a small blue frame and inside the frame was a picture—me, Neeka and D sitting on the stoop, smiling at the camera. D's half smile making her seem like she was asking the world, *Can I trust you?* Neeka's crazy face all eyes and knowledge—something deep in her smile. Like she was old. Like a part of her was grown-up already. And me? I was sitting between my girls, looking away from the camera—off down the street somewhere. That day, when Mama took the picture, I'd been watching the little girls try to jump double Dutch. But that's not what it looked like. In the picture I look like I'm looking to where I'm going to. Sitting on that stoop, but already gone from here.

I put the picture on the small shelf above my bed.

"It's great, Ma. Thank you."

"There's twenty dollars behind the picture," Mama said. She smiled, knowing I'd lose my mind with that much money.

But I didn't. There could have been a quarter behind there—or a penny. Or nothing at all. The picture was enough. The picture was *always.*

"You can treat your girls to lunch."

I nodded but didn't say anything for a long time.

"I hope it means that it's a dollar for each year they're gonna be my girls," I said. "I hope it's me and Neeka and D always."

"Hush, girl," Mama said. "You know it will be."

That morning, the first morning of my teenage life, I believed her.

CHAPTER THIRTEEN

A summer storm passed over the night before we all took the bus up to see Tash on Saturday, hard rain and thunder all through the night. Hot winds blowing everywhere. I had spent the night over Neeka's house and by the time we woke up, the rain had stopped and everything felt quiet and clean and cooler somehow. Neeka's dad had to work and couldn't go with us. The night before, I'd watched him press some bills inside

Miss Irene's hand and say softly, *You give that boy my love, you hear.*

You know I will, Miss Irene said. And they stood there, holding each other. Miss Irene was tall. She was too skinny but she was pretty anyway. Most people looked surprised when they found out how many kids she had, but she'd just laugh and say, *You know black don't crack. I'm older than I look.*

When they let go of each other, Miss Irene wiped her eyes and whispered, *Lord, give me just a little piece of strength more.*

Me and Neeka were up before the sun even rose helping Miss Irene get the little ones dressed. Neeka's twin sisters were almost four and acting like fools—screaming, spinning in circles and doing everything except what Neeka told them to do. I had to tell them to put on their shoes five times before Miss Irene came into the room, pulling her belt out from her pants and swearing she'd use it. After that, the twins jumped to it, crying like their mama had already beat their behinds.

"Y'all don't ever want to listen to nobody," Neeka said. She'd woke up in a bad mood and her pinched-up face stayed that way all through breakfast.

"I can't stand oatmeal," Neeka said, pushing the bowl away.

I didn't like oatmeal either, but I knew it'd be hours before we ate again and I wasn't trying to be hungry on a long bus ride. Miss Irene had made a ton of food, but we weren't going to get to eat it until we were sitting down with Tash.

Neeka's twin brothers, Albert and Emmett, were reading comic books and shoveling oatmeal into their mouths like someone was gonna steal it if they didn't get it down their throats.

Neeka turned her evil mood on them.

"You two need to stop acting like there ain't no food up in this house. I know you didn't wake up that hungry."

"I know I didn't hear you say 'ain't,' " Miss Irene called from her bedroom.

Neeka's face got so evil, she looked about ready to explode.

"Mind your business," Emmett said. "You not the boss of nobody. If I feel like eating this stuff standing on my head, you can't do anything about it."

"Me too," Albert said.

They were ten and close to being taller than Neeka. She made a face at them but didn't say anything else.

The girls giggled and went back to feeding each other oatmeal and saying, "Good, baby. You such a good baby."

Tash's prison was a three-hour bus ride from where we lived. But to get to the bus that went there once a month, we had to take two trains. In the subway, I held the girls' hands. Neeka was supposed to be keeping an eye on Albert and Emmett and Miss Irene and Jayjones carried the food and stuff we were taking up to Tash.

Once we got on the first subway, Neeka took a seat far away from everybody and pulled a book out of her bag. She stuck her face in it and didn't look up again until our stop came and Miss Irene said, "Girl, you better get your behind up and help us get these kids off this train!"

While we waited for the next train, Miss Irene fussed with Neeka.

"You can wake up in a bad mood if you want to, but you better act like you're part of this family."

"Can't *stand* this family," Neeka mumbled, turning her head away from her moms to cut her eyes.

"Well, that's too bad, because you're stuck with us now," her mama said.

"Nobody told you to have all these kids."

I took a breath. Neeka was about to get slapped right out in public. But Miss Irene just smiled.

"I guess I should have stopped before I got to you, huh?"

The train came and Neeka pushed the boys ahead of her into it. It was an East Side train, which meant it was filled with white people. I watched them trying not to look at our loud, raggedy bunch, but they couldn't seem to help themselves. Neeka glared at whoever she could make eye contact with until it was time to get off again.

"Why you so evil?" I asked when we were all settled on the bus and surrounded by mostly black people again.

Neeka had taken the window seat. I was in the aisle seat

and the girls were across from us, losing their minds over not having to sit with any big kids. I knew before the end of the bus ride Miss Irene would be over that and have separated them. But for now, me and Neeka had some halfway private, halfway quiet time.

Neeka leaned her head against the window. The bus was a Trailways, so the seats were soft but it smelled like the blue liquid they put in the toilet bowls. I'd only been up with them to see Tash two times, and both times we'd sat in the front, away from the bathroom so it didn't smell as bad.

"You can't even find your Big Purpose up in this family. Can't get your head straight."

"Your head looks fine to me, Neek. You look nice today."

She did. Her hair was greased and braided so that it looked clean and shiny. She was wearing a pair of jeans and a white T-shirt with a light brown jacket over it. She'd never even had one pimple and I looked at her skin, surprised all over again by how beautifully brown it was.

"Not my outside head. My *inside* head. D's already close to knowing what her Big Purpose is—she's up in her house with just Flo and got all that time to think and stuff. And you get to be just with your mama or by yourself or whatever. But I wake up and there's kids and noise and my mama telling me to do this and do that. These ain't even my kids!" She glared over at the twins. They were looking at us and both stuck their tongue out at her.

"There's like no place where it could be empty and quiet. It's all this noise. All the time."

She leaned her head back against the window. The city was disappearing and outside I could see trees and patches of grass.

"You should come stay at my house more," I said. But I didn't really want that. I loved the noise and craziness of Neeka's house. Most days, I wished we could switch places.

"It's not the same," Neeka said to the window. "Sometimes I think maybe I should just do something wrong—get sent to some juvie place where they lock you down alone in your room."

"Yeah, but then no matter how much planning you did, you wouldn't be able to do nothing about it. 'Cause you'd be on lockdown."

"I know," Neeka said, her voice so soft and sad, I didn't even know what else to say.

She blew a breath on the window, then wrote a D in it. I watched her stare at the D for a few minutes until it faded. It was July and outside the sun was just beginning to come up. The sky was blue and pink and beautiful. The air-conditioning was on hard and I wished I'd brought a jacket for the bus.

"You ever wonder if people gonna remember your name?" Neeka said.

"Like how?"

"Like my name's Daneeka L. Jones. But everybody calls me Neeka and most people don't even know that my real name begins with a D. Or what the L is for."

"Lucy," I said. "Because your daddy used to watch Charlie Brown a lot and his favorite person was Lucy."

I saw Neeka smile a bit. "Yeah. *You* know it. And some *teachers* know it. And the kids at school and some people on the block. And my family. But that's it."

"That's kinda a lot, Neeka. I mean—that's like fifty people already and you're not even grown yet. You figure fifty people, say every couple of years, by the time you die, it's gonna be in the thousands or something, right?"

"There's millions of people in the world, though. And more getting born every day. And some of them blow up—like Tupac did. I think that's why he's so cool by me, because he didn't come from any rich people like a lot of those celebrities be coming from—with their mamas or their daddies already movie stars." Neeka leaned her head against the window. "I mean his parents were out there being Black Panthers and whatnot, but they was struggling too. Didn't always have money. Didn't always have food."

Neeka looked at me. "I want to blow up. Have people knowing my name. I want to walk inside a subway car and have white people be giving me big respect instead of looking at me and my family like we some kind of circus act or something."

Someone was eating something good—I could smell the flavors drifting through the bus. I could hear wax paper crinkling and an old lady's voice saying, *Take a piece of this, honey. I know you hungry.*

"I want people to see me," Neeka said. "And know I'm *somebody*."

"Too bad you can't sing," I said.

"I can sing."

"Not good, though."

Neeka jabbed me in the side but she was smiling.

"You know what I want to do," she said, her voice getting real low. "I been thinking about it lots."

"What?" I leaned a little closer to her.

"You can't laugh at me."

"Do I look like I'm gonna laugh, Neek?"

"I want to teach at a college. I want to be a college professor."

I felt myself starting to laugh, but Neeka's face got real serious, like she was daring me to.

"What are you gonna teach?"

Neeka turned back to the window and shrugged. "Maybe like math or law or something. I want to be in one of those big lecture rooms like you see in the colleges on TV. Where there's all these kids and they're listening to every single word the professor is saying. And the professor has those little half glasses that make him look real smart and every time a student asks him a question, he knows the answer."

"Don't you have to go to law school or something to teach law?"

Neeka shrugged. "I don't care."

"You'd be good at it, Neek. You're always arguing with Jayjones. And usually you be winning."

Neeka smiled. Then, real fast, her smile went away.

"If I was a lawyer already," she said, "Tash wouldn't be in jail probably. That lawyer didn't even know what he was doing because my brother didn't do nothing wrong. That's what's so messed up."

"I know."

"Tash didn't know that guy was gonna rob anybody. Else he wouldn't have been with him."

"I know."

Tash was doing time for an assault crime he didn't commit. Neeka always said he was doing time for being in the wrong place at the wrong time. Everybody—except the judge and the jury—knew Tash wasn't the kind of guy to assault anybody, unless they were messing with us. He always threatened, since we were tiny, to slice in half anybody that tried to mess with me and Neeka. And even though I'd never even seen him with a knife, I believed him. But he wasn't in jail for slicing somebody who was messing with us.

"We all know," Neeka said. "But we ain't the ones that need to be knowing. Us knowing don't do anybody any good."

I started to say *I know* again but didn't. Knew I didn't have to.

Outside, the sun was up now. There were trees everywhere and the big green leaves on them looked heavy, like they wanted to pull the branches down. Every now and then, we passed a farm. I'd learned in school that the high dome-looking things were called silos. There was something so beautiful about the way they looked with the sun rising up over them and the farm looking all quiet and the cows barely moving—it felt like somebody somewhere was making the world a promise, a promise that there'd be a new day and that we'd have milk to drink. Always.

Seemed wrong to be seeing all that beauty outside with Neeka feeling sad and us going to see Tash in jail. Where Tash was, the walls were all painted the same sorry gray and there was always the sound of somebody yelling. The windows were real small and had bars on them. I couldn't even imagine how it felt to look out on a beautiful new day through some bars.

I put my head on Neeka's bony shoulder and we stared out the window, watching the farms move by us. Someone had put on some music—oldies songs. Behind me, Albert was still sitting next to Emmett and both of them were reading Emmett's comic books. The girls had fallen asleep on each other. Behind them, Jayjones and Miss Irene were sitting together. Miss Irene was doing a crossword puzzle and Jayjones was listening to his Walkman and staring out the window.

"It's all quiet now," I said to Neeka. "You can start working on planning your Big Purpose."

Neeka stared out the window. And nodded.

CHAPTER FOURTEEN

The loudest sound in the world is the soft click of prison gates locking behind you.

Maybe it's how final it is—the loud slam of the gate, then the quick, gentle click. Then the scary feeling of it all being forever.

So many gates slamming shut. So many locks clicking. One after the other until you're all the way inside.

And the only way out is at the hands of a prison guard, who has to press a button. And turn a key. Then press another button and turn another key. All the while staring at each of you. And you know what he's thinking:

Remember this place good, y'all. We got a spot waiting for you.

CHAPTER FIFTEEN

"Shoes and belts off," the guards yelled.

We moved down the line slowly, waiting while the guards went through Miss Irene's bag, searched inside the girls' shoes, glared at Emmett and Albert and Jayjones. Albert wore wire-frame glasses and the guards made him take them off and put them through the metal detector. Albert looked tiny and a little afraid without his glasses on. He looked around the room real quick, then

rubbed his eyes. His glasses were kinda thick, so I knew without them he couldn't see much. When the guard handed
them back, Albert whispered, *Thank you*, wiped them off on
his shirt and put them back on.

Then when we were all signed in, the final gate slammed
behind us and we joined a bunch of other families in a big
room as we waited for Tash to be brought down.

All around us, people were hugging and kissing each
other. I watched one old-looking woman hold a young guy
like she'd never let him go, her eyes closed tight but the
tears pushing through anyway. I heard him say, *Ma, don't cry.
Ma, please don't cry*. But the tears kept falling like they never
planned to stop.

A young couple across from us pressed their foreheads
together, a boy about three years old dancing circles around
them.

The room was crowded and hot and loud. I stared at the
door where Tash would come through.

The first thing I noticed about him this time was how
skinny he'd gotten. Tash wasn't a big guy to begin with, but
in the months since I'd last seen him, the tiny bit of meat
beneath his cheekbones had disappeared and his beige uniform hung all big on him. But when he saw us, he let go of
that big Tash smile and inside that skinny face I could see the
Tash I'd known forever.

"Girl, you are *not* stepping up in here looking like Miss
Thang now, is you?" Tash grinned and gave Neeka a big hug.

"All tall and almost-grown. Come here and let Tash spin you around."

Then he was hugging everyone and everyone was hugging him back and I felt the same old stupid huge stone rise up in my throat and the same stupid tears coming down. Neeka was crying too. So was Miss Irene. I saw Jayjones pull his hands across his eyes.

"Don't even," Tash said, waving his skinny finger at us. "You know this girl is getting out of here soon. Don't come up in here crying now. I ain't having it."

We found a place at a long table in the back and Miss Irene started pulling food from the shopping bags. There was roasted chicken, mac and cheese, corn bread, potato salad, salad and corn. She'd brought paper plates and plastic spoons because they wouldn't allow plastic forks for some dumb reason. After we'd all filled up our plates, Tash started telling us, between tiny girlie bites, how he was getting out soon.

Jayjones was sitting directly across from him. He just kept looking at Tash and grinning, like he couldn't believe he was getting to be right across from his big brother.

"Mama, when you talked to the lawyer, he ain't tell you about them reversing it?"

Miss Irene chewed her chicken slowly and swallowed. "Tash, you know I don't understand half the things that man be saying. Only thing he seems to know how to say so real people can understand is how much to write his check for!"

Tash smiled, lowering his eyes slowly and waving his hand at Miss Irene. "Hush, girl!" he said. "Don't we know that for a fact."

Miss Irene nodded. She glanced over at Emmett and Albert, then back at Tash. Miss Irene didn't like Tash acting sissyish around the boys. Tash saw her look and tried to sit up a little bit straighter. Emmett and Albert didn't seem to care, though. Mostly they grinned when Tash talked.

"Well, it's all working out," he said. "And the way I'm thinking, I should be out of here by the end of summer. But you know we won't know till we get there. And when I get out of here, first thing I'm gonna be working on is finding a way to pay you and Daddy back for all these . . . these *legal* fees."

This time, Miss Irene waved her hand. "Just work on coming home, Tash."

"I'm for real, Mama. You know how many more rich Negroes there'd be if we wasn't all the time trying to pay off some lawyer or bailing a brother out. That's one thing I'm truly guilty of—giving hard-earned money to *the man*. One person mess up, legal system got the whole family on lockdown."

Tash looked around the room and rolled his eyes.

"Ain't just black folks either," he said. "Look at us."

We all looked. There were people everywhere.

"Puerto Ricans and white guys," Tash said. "Indian brothers over there and some Chinese guys over in the corner there. Most people stick with they own kind, but we all in the same place—doing the same thing—*time.* And I'm telling you, time is a *bee-atch.*"

"You really coming home, man?" Jayjones asked. He shook Tash's arm and made him turn back toward us.

"Yeah, man!" Tash said, deepening his voice to imitate Jayjones. "I'm really coming home, man."

Jayjones grinned and took a big bite of his mac and cheese.

Tash ate delicately and laughed whenever one of us did or said something halfway funny. A long time ago, he'd started locking his hair and now the locks were long and he'd pulled them back into a ponytail. His eyebrows had always been tweezed perfectly when he was on the outside, but they'd grown in now. He and Neeka had the same dark, big eyes. The same long lashes. The same long straight nose and pretty lips. I stared at Tash. When he caught me staring, he winked at me and smiled. When we were little, we'd beg and beg until Tash did our nails or hair, and when me and Neeka walked out onto the block, seemed everybody we came across had something good to say about how we looked.

"You and Neeka sure are growing up before a sister's eyes."

"Tash . . . " Miss Irene said.

"Before a *brother's* eyes," Tash said.

"And you getting skinny," Neeka said. "You okay?"

"Heck no, I ain't okay," Tash said. "I'm in jail and I'm

a *queen*. You know that means a sister's gotta fight for her right to party. But no, I don't have the Monster—this body is HIV free and staying that way. Don't be a gay boy and get skinny—people start giving you the death look." He made a terrified-looking face, then smiled. "I'm still walking and talking and eating Mama's cooking. That's all you gotta worry about, Miss Neeka!"

"Tash, you know I don't like—"

"Mama, I'm in jail. Give me little bit of joy. I ain't hurting nobody. I ain't *never* tried to hurt nobody who wasn't hurting me first. I know who I am and you know who I am and every one of these kids knows who I am. Ain't that good enough?"

Miss Irene took a deep breath and put her hands in her lap. She looked down and didn't say anything for a moment. I could feel everybody at the table holding their breath. We'd had this same talk the last time we came to visit Tash.

"Ain't I good enough?" Tash said, softer.

Miss Irene dabbed at her eyes with a napkin and nodded. "You know you are, baby. You know you are."

"Then let me be this way, Mama. Let me be this way."

After another minute passed, Miss Irene lifted her head and nodded. "Well, you don't have to just be skin and bones being *that way*," she said, piling more food on Tash's plate. "Have some more of this mac and cheese, baby."

Neeka looked at me. The moment was over and we all let out a breath.

The girls got up and ran around the table a couple of times. Jayjones gave them some money and they headed over to the vending machines.

"They don't know how to work those," Emmett said, getting up to chase after them. Albert just watched him go, then moved a little bit closer to Tash. Tash put his arm around Albert and kissed the top of his head. Tash was eleven years older than Albert and Emmett. Albert had been a little bit sickly as a baby, so Tash used to sit up with him late at night, telling him stories about how great the world was and how he needed to get himself healthy so he could enjoy it. Albert didn't remember any of it. At least not in his head. But he loved Tash more than anything.

"What's happening in the world of basketball?" Tash said, turning to Jayjones. "And please make it interesting, 'cause you know I can't stand sports."

Jayjones grinned. "I shot three hundred and fifty baskets the other day. My arms be aching, yo. But I just keep going."

"Especially if a girl's watching," Neeka said.

Jayjones ignored her.

"Got a good feeling about going pro. I mean, you don't be seeing a lot of us getting there, but I got the advantage because my grades is good and I'm still growing and stuff."

"Your grades just *okay*," Neeka said. "I wouldn't say *good*."

Jayjones just looked at her, but Miss Irene told her to hush.

"College first," Miss Irene said, working on a tough piece of chicken, trying hard to cut through it with the plastic spoon. "They come around making all kinds of offers, but you tear up a knee and three years later they won't even remember your name."

Neeka looked at me.

"I *know*, Ma," Jayjones said, sounding annoyed. "I got all plans to go to college first. That's why I been trying to pull down good grades!"

"You really be just standing there shooting the ball into the basket like that?" Tash said.

"Yup," Neeka answered for Jayjones. "Over and over and over and over. The sun goes up and he's standing there shooting. Sun comes down and he still standing there shooting. Snow. Rain. Don't matter. Like a dude that's lost his mind."

"Genius *is* crazy," Jayjones said. "That's what everybody be saying. If you got any kind of genius in you, it's like right on that line between being real brilliant and real crazy. I got genius in me when it comes to ball."

"Nah," Neeka said. "I think you just got crazy in you."

It seemed to get noisier in the common room with so many other families around us. Down the table, a young girl was holding a small baby. The guy she was visiting didn't look much older than Jayjones. The woman beside her looked older, like she could be one of their moms. When the baby started crying, the girl took a bottle out of her bag.

I heard her say, *You lucky, baby. The guards almost took your formula.*

Across the room, Emmett and the girls were walking from vending machine to vending machine. Some had coffee. Others had sandwiches or candy or chips in them. They took their sweet time deciding what they wanted.

"What's the first thing you gonna do when you get home, Tash?" I asked.

"Girl, you know I'm gonna get my hair twisted, make myself a cute drink and get myself over to the river and see my people!"

The river was where all the gay guys hung out. Sometimes Tash took me and Neeka with him when he went to hang with his "girls." I loved going because the other queens always made such a fuss over us, telling us how beautiful we were and how we'd grow up to give somebody "fever" one day.

"Some of the children came to see me last week and they were like, *Girl, how is you living up in* here?!"

I laughed, trying to imagine Tash's queenie friends looking around at the gray walls and dirty floor and barred-up windows.

Tash laughed too.

"They been coming up in here for all this time—and every single time they walk up in here, they acting like it's their first."

The children. That's what Tash had always called his gay friends. When me and Neeka were finally old enough to ask why, Tash said, *You know what they say. Sunday's child is happy, bright and gay! So we are most definitely Sunday's children.*

"Jayjones," Tash said, getting serious. "Don't ever get yourself locked up."

Jayjones rolled his eyes. "You tell me that every time, man."

"I'm serious, Jayjones," Tash said, raising his finger at him. "You don't ever want to get your freedom taken away like this. They try to take your *soul* up in this place and you gotta fight hard to keep you inside of you." He looked at Albert. "You tell Emmett the same thing, Al."

Albert nodded but didn't say anything.

Tash turned back to Jayjones.

"And you tell your gangsta homies and you tell anybody that don't know that there ain't nothing cute about this place." Tash's voice got wobbly and he pressed his fingers against his mouth and closed his eyes.

"I'm not coming here, Tash," Jayjones said real soft. "Count on it, man."

"I am counting on it," Tash said. "People talk you into stuff you'll be regretting to your grave. I lay on my piece of a cot and I go over that night again and again in my head. And when I have my dreams, I'm not anywhere near where I was the night they arrested me. I'm on a beach or in my apartment or at some fancy restaurant eating lobster. And then I open my eyes and the bell's ringing for us to get up and get busy. Every day it's the same old day in this place, Jayjones. Every day, the same old tired day."

"I shoot baskets," Jayjones said quietly. "I shoot baskets and the whole world drops away."

He looked at Tash like it was only the two of them in the room, only the two of them in the whole wide world. "Everything that's real hard disappears."

Tash nodded, then looked down at Albert. "And what about you, Al? What do you be doing?"

Albert smiled. He readjusted his glasses on his face and shrugged.

"Not talk. I tell you that much," Neeka said.

"Well, why should he if he's got you to talk for him." Tash squeezed Albert's shoulder. "Neeka speak for you most of the time?"

Albert nodded and pointed his chin to over where Emmett was standing by a vending machine with candy in it.

"I know *he* talks enough for quadruplets!" Tash said. "Well, you rest your voice and grow your brain if you need to, little brother. Your mama got so many kids, she needs some quiet ones in the bunch."

At the other end of the room, a guy was taking pictures of families. Tash said it cost five dollars and asked Miss Irene if she wanted a group shot.

Miss Irene's hair was in a French braid pinned up at the back of her neck. She smoothed it back and adjusted the bobby pins holding it in place before answering.

"I'm not saying this to criticize you, Tash. But I don't expect any of the other children to ever end up in jail."

She shot a look at Jayjones, who started to say something but didn't. Maybe it was the look Miss Irene gave him.

"Once you come home, I don't ever plan to take that bus up here to see anybody ever again."

She got up and started clearing our plates into the now empty shopping bag. I stood up to help her. The blue jeans she was wearing had creases down the front and the light blue T-shirt looked new. She had two gold bangles on one wrist and a watch on the other. Her arms were the same pretty light brown as Neeka's. Mama always talked about how well put together Miss Irene was and now I got it.

"I'm saying this to you," Miss Irene said, "because I don't want any pictures commemorating your time here. I don't ever want to look at a photo and say, 'Yeah, that's when Tash was in jail.' Because the minute you come home, baby, I'm gonna forget all about this time."

"Amen," Tash said. "Amen a hundred times."

The photographer was taking a picture of the couple who had their heads pressed together earlier. The man was holding the little boy in his arms and smiling. The woman still looked sad, though. *Say cheese, Mommy,* the little boy said. *God is watching you.*

Maybe he'd heard that from his mother a hundred times. Maybe more than that.

Emmett and the girls came back over and Emmett handed Tash a package of peanut M&M's.

"I always remember that you like the peanut ones," he said.

Tash gave him a hug. "Thanks, E."

Emmett smiled and sat down on the other side of Tash. When he wasn't looking, Tash made a face at me and mouthed, *I hate peanut M&M's.* Then he gave Emmett another squeeze and popped two in his mouth, making a face as he chewed them.

Tash was always falling in love with guys that didn't want to be with him. Maybe that's why he got caught up with Sly. For a while, Sly was cool with being on the block and around the neighborhood with Tash. But maybe that was all part of the whole setup.

Tash played the piano at church, and when his fingers touched the piano keys, it was like magic was taking over the whole place, making it all soft and holy and different. When Tash played the piano, church ladies dabbed at their eyes, threw their hands in the air and said, *Well . . . !* in this way that people do. It meant *What more can I say*. It meant *God is good every day*. It meant *Ain't this all something?*

Tash's fingers were long and light brown, and sometimes when he'd go just to practice and nobody else would be in the church, me and Neeka used to go with him. We'd stand around that church piano and sing all kinds of songs. Neeka's voice was high and pretty and mine was kind of low. The one time D came with us—right before Tash got arrested—she sang too. Her voice was just regular, soft and shy, but Tash said we all three together made a perfect harmony. *Get y'all some wigs, you could be the next Supremes*, he said.

The guy who'd taught Tash to play was named Randall. When Tash was a little boy, rumor had it that Randall took Tash's hand, studied Tash's long fingers and said, *Music is going to save you, baby. Ain't nobody out there can take your talent away.* Maybe Randall saw something in Tash nobody else could see yet. Maybe he knew that Tash would need some saving. Maybe that's why he'd started teaching him to play piano—so Tash could walk into that church and give people music and then nobody could say anything about any of the other stuff.

Tash used to tell us the story. *Legendary,* he'd say, throwing his head back. *My talent is legendary.* Randall was old now and he was kind of a sissy boy like Tash.

The night Tash got arrested, Sly had called Tash to meet

him at a club near where we lived. Sly lived out in Brooklyn, but he'd been hanging with Tash for a few months by then. Tash had first met Sly at some club in Manhattan and nothing about Sly said gay boy. He wore his jeans way low and kept his hair in braids and a gold chain with SLY in thick diamonds around his neck. The few times I'd seen him and Tash talking, I'd felt cold and a little bit scared. When I asked Tash why Sly wasn't like him, he said, *Girl, gay comes in all kinds. Don't even try to recognize just by looking. Sly's truly one of the children, no matter how thug he tries to be.*

The night Tash met Sly, Tash got a few drinks in him and started talking about Randall—about how good he'd been to Tash and how he had a baby grand piano inside his house. Randall hadn't been rich, but he had a nice house with beautiful rugs, African statues all around and pretty pictures on the wall. The few times I'd gone there with Tash and Neeka, I'd been happy just to sit in the living room and look at all Randall's stuff.

I sure wouldn't mind hearing you play that piano, Sly had said. *And making sure this Randall guy ain't somebody I need to be jealous about.*

Sometimes when I was lying in my room, watching the glow-in-the-dark stars on my ceiling start coming to life, I couldn't help but think about good and bad people. I couldn't help thinking about how it is that somebody like Sly met up with somebody like Tash. About how somebody like Tash fell in love with somebody like Sly. I didn't understand love, the way it let you not see all that junk that people be showing right up front. Seemed Tash never even noticed the way Sly always showed up alone, didn't have no boys or no girls with him. You needed your boys. You needed your girls. Everybody knew that.

A few months after they met, Sly and Tash and some guy Sly said *was a good friend and liked music too* ended up at Randall's house. Tash said Randall was happy to have the company and even played a few songs himself. *Wasn't until I sat down to play this Vandross song, "So Amazing." And I'm all into that song because that's what I'm feeling—like Sly was all about me and it was amazing, you know. To think somebody loves you like that.*

The first time Tash told us the story, he was sitting in Rikers Island and me, Neeka and Miss Irene had gone to see him. His face was still swollen from the beating Sly and his friend had given him and his hands shook as he spoke. I'd known Tash all my life and that was the first time I'd ever seen him cry.

"*It's so amazing to be loved,*" Tash sang softly. "*I'd follow you to the moon and stars above.*" He stopped singing and stared over our heads. *That's when things went crazy,* he whispered.

By the time the cops got there, Sly and his boy had beaten Randall and Tash real bad and the apartment had been turned all inside out. Randall wasn't conscious and the only one there to tell the story was Tash. *They beat me too,* Tash kept screaming. *They beat me too.* But he'd brought Sly and the guy into the house, and Randall wasn't clear enough to know whether Tash was one of the good guys or one of the bad. And when they caught Sly and the other guy, they both said Tash was in on it too. In the end, Sly, Tash and the other guy all ended up in jail.

Miss Irene's church friends took up collections for Tash and for Randall. But by the time Randall was well enough to get out of the hospital, some of his people from down south came and got him and took him back with them.

Randall's memory had gotten real bad with the beating and he just knew that it was three guys and somebody was beating on him and somebody was screaming. But he didn't know who was who anymore.

Tash spent a few weeks at Rikers Island, which wasn't as bad as the big prison. Rikers Island was kind of like a holding place, where people who hadn't done really, really bad stuff or people who were waiting to see which way things were gonna go ended up. But some guy started messing with Tash at Rikers. That wasn't good. *You let one mess with you*, Tash told us later, *you'll have a whole lot of guys messing with you.* So Tash got a knife somewhere and cut the guy in a few, as he told it, *choice places.*

You know this girl don't play, he said.

In the end, Randall was getting on a bus heading down south and Tash was on a bus heading upstate to do time.

Randall told me these hands was gonna save me, Tash told us, months later—the first time we visited him upstate. *And I ain't gonna stop believing that they will one day.*

CHAPTER SEVENTEEN

It was late when we got home on Saturday night. Miss Irene asked Jayjones to walk me across the street, and when we got to my house, I was shocked as anything to see D sitting on the stairs, her arms folded across her chest, her hair out and wild over her back and shoulders.

"Where y'all been all day," she asked, looking up at us. "It's almost nine o'clock."

"Girl," I said. "Flo know you out this late?"

Even though it was hot as anything out, D shivered.

"Flo don't own me," D said, glaring off at nothing. "She just my foster mom. Foster mamas take you in . . . " She put up her hands. "And let you go."

Jayjones started to sit beside her, but D gave him such a fierce look that he got right back up and said, "Later, y'all."

When we got upstairs, the lights were mostly out, which meant Mama was sleeping. D followed me into the kitchen, where Mama had left a night-light on and a plate of food for me. I asked D if she was hungry and she nodded. I wasn't, so I pushed the plate of food over and she sat down at the table and started eating.

I turned on the small lamp we had on the countertop. In the goldish light it gave off, D looked old and tired and beautiful. She ate slowly, letting out deep breaths every now and then.

"What's up, girl?" I asked.

"Could I spend the night here, tonight?" D looked up at me and waited. She was wearing a green T-shirt with a huge D on the front. A thick silver bracelet on her wrist that I'd never seen before.

"Flo gonna let you spend the night?"

D rolled her eyes. "I told you, that lady don't own me."

I heard footsteps and when I looked up, Neeka was standing in the doorway, her eyes wide as anything. She'd had keys to our house forever and used them whenever she came over. I couldn't remember the last time Neeka had knocked or rang our bell.

"My mama says I got ten minutes," Neeka said. "So talk fast, D."

Neeka came into the kitchen, leaned against the counter and folded her arms.

"But talk soft because my moms is sleeping," I said.

D took another bite of her food and pushed the plate away. It was almost empty.

"Y'all really want the real scoop?" she asked.

Me and Neeka looked at each other, then both of us nodded.

D took another deep breath. When she started talking, she wasn't looking at us—just staring past us into someplace in the hallway darkness.

"When I was in the group home," she said, her voice real low, "I heard the counselors having a meeting one time. We was supposed to be up in our rooms, but the rooms were small and smelly and there was always some drama going on, so I'd snuck downstairs and was sitting behind the couch. I guess I was about seven because I remember I was small enough to squeeze behind that couch."

She blinked, then leaned on her fist and stared down at the table, tracing tiny patterns on it with her finger.

"I was reading a magazine, just sitting there—not really trying to be listening to their meeting but I could hear it anyway. Mostly they was talking about junk I didn't care about, but then I heard this counselor say, *Why do we keep calling them homeless and foster and runaways. These kids ain't none of that*, he said. *They're throwaway kids. Their parents don't* want *them.*"

I could feel the floor shake from the vibration of D's leg jiggling under the table.

"You ain't no throwaway, D," Neeka said. "I bet there's a million mamas would want you."

D shrugged. She didn't look up, just took another breath and kept on.

"I heard him say that and I knew the next foster situation I ended up in, I was gonna make work no matter what. 'Cause I wasn't gonna be no throwaway kid."

She looked at me. "I wasn't gonna be like Brenda's baby."

I nodded, my head spinning. She was our friend and we didn't really know her. Every minute it was like there was a little bit more about her that made everything so ... so complicated. I couldn't even imagine trying to walk through the world after somebody said I was a throwaway kid.

"So when Social Services said they had a family that wanted a little girl, I scrubbed my face and ironed my clothes and had a counselor do my hair. I wanted to be ... " She frowned, like she was just remembering. "I wanted to be *perfect*. The mama in that family couldn't have kids, and they wanted to buy a house, so they had all these foster kids because you get money when you take in foster kids. I don't know how much, but it helped them buy that house and all."

Neeka and me looked at each other again but didn't say anything. It'd been almost two years and we were finally starting to get somewhere on the history of D's life.

"Well, they got their house and then she got pregnant and they found out it was gonna be twins, so they started getting rid of the foster kids—one by one. I was one of the first ones to go. So I went back to the group home and I stayed there for a while.

"I was in a whole lot of other places when I was a kid, and sometimes I was with my mama and sometimes I wasn't."

Neeka couldn't hold herself back anymore.

"Where *is* your mama?" She asked. "She live somewhere close by?"

D looked up at Neeka and shrugged. "Sometimes she do. Sometimes she don't. I think her Big Purpose got all scattered or something, so she goes chasing after it."

"How long you been with Flo?" I asked.

"Going on three and a half years. Flo's been the longest foster mama. Even though she be acting all bent out of shape about how I dress and making me go to church and all that nonsense, she takes care of me. She lets me roam because she says, the way she figures it, I been around so much, I must know the city just like the back of my hand. So as long as I show up at that door when I'm supposed to, she lets me go. And she's not trying to buy a house or have any kids or anything."

118

D took another deep breath. I could see she was trying hard not to cry. I got a paper towel from the roll on the counter and handed it to her. We had been whispering, and when nobody was talking, the quiet sounded louder than anything. The kitchen was hot and smelled like garlic. Any other time, I would have loved the smell. But that night, it made me a little bit nauseous.

"Now Flo's telling me my moms wants to give it another shot," D said. She wiped her eyes with the paper towel.

"Said the state and the city and everybody thinks she's ready. Said she got a place upstate somewhere and there's a room for me and all. Flo's letting me go that easy. And I guess that's right because I ain't hers really, right? But I ain't my mama's either 'cause she been so off and on for so long."

I went over to D and rubbed her back. She was crying softly now.

"I always thought I wanted that—to have my moms back. To be living with her. To have a room that was just made for me, a house I could be taking my friends to and all . . ."

"But we're Three the Hard Way," Neeka said. She looked confused and hurt. "You're our girl, D."

"I know. Y'all mine. I feel like I keep trying to do the right thing and somebody always gotta make the new rules for me—get to tell me how to do my hair, what clothes to wear, where to sleep, where I'm gonna be living."

"You really leaving, D?" Neeka asked.

D nodded. "Flo say if it don't work out, I can come back and live with her."

D leaned back against me, her head on my stomach.

"But it don't go like that."

"You're a part of us, D," Neeka said.

But D just looked at her and gave her that crooked half smile. And everything in those beautiful green eyes said, *I don't believe you but hope so.*

A week passed. And then another. We didn't hear from D and she didn't come around. Summer was getting close to being over and me and Neeka went shopping for school clothes with Mama and Miss Irene. We got the news that Tash really was coming home, and the whole way on the trains to Manhattan and in the stores, Miss Irene and Mama talked about how good it would be to have him out of jail.

CHAPTER EIGHTEEN

When we got to Thirty-fourth Street where all the stores were, me and Neeka walked slowly through the aisles, looking at jeans and shirts and cute skirts we'd wear come the school year. We bought a few matching outfits even though people probably wouldn't mistake us for sisters anymore. I was almost a full head taller than Neeka now and I still had my cornrows. Neeka had relaxed her hair so that it was bone straight and hanging around her shoulders.

Miss Irene had gotten a babysitter for the twins, and Jayjones was taking some basketball lessons from a private coach he'd gotten with his KFC money. It was nice to be walking through the stores with just Mama, Miss Irene and Neeka without all the kids running wild around us. If D had been there, it would have been perfect.

"You think she's already gone?" I asked Neeka.

We were trying on shoes. When the salesman brought out the first pair, Mama shook her head.

"Take those back," she said to the salesman. "They're too high. That child's thirteen, not thirty."

I rolled my eyes and tried on a flatter pair.

"I don't know," Neeka said. "I hope not. You can't just be disappearing like that on your girls."

"Remember when we first met her," I said. "How she just showed up and then she was gone and we didn't know if she'd come back again."

Neeka nodded.

"But she came back. And when she came back, she stayed." She crossed her arms over her chest and let out a breath.

"She stayed," she said again, softer.

"Crazy how we don't even have digits or an address for her," I said. "And who knew there was like two hundred Fosters in Queens alone."

"Yeah," Neeka said. "How we gonna be her girls like that and not even know the *basic* stuff you needed to know about her."

She put on the shoes the salesman brought, took a few steps in the shoes, then turned and walked back toward me.

Miss Irene shook her head.

"Oh, Lord, y'all sure are growing up," she said.

Mama looked at me and Neeka. And slowly nodded.

CHAPTER NINETEEN

September came up on us quickly. It had gotten cool and cloudy out and me and Neeka sat on her stairs wearing our new jeans and sweaters. Neeka had just gotten Tupac's tape and we were listening to it on her Walkman, each of us with one earphone over our ear. It was hard to listen to it and not think about D.

Upstairs, Miss Irene was getting the place together for Tash, who was coming home. She'd made a whole lot of food and even got some helium balloons from Party City. There was a red tablecloth on the table and red plastic plates and forks because that was Tash's favorite color. All morning long, Miss Irene had been humming to herself and smiling, happier than I'd seen her in a long time.

Jayjones and Neeka's dad had gone to meet Tash at the bus station, but me and Neeka had stayed behind, helping out. Then, when the Neeka's sisters started acting the fool, pulling on the balloons and climbing under the table, me and Neeka decided it was more peaceful down on the stairs.

"These beats are tight," Neeka said, moving her head to the music.

The album had hit double platinum and everybody either had a real copy or a bootleg. Neeka's was bootleg—Jayjones had made a tape of a tape, so it was a little bit fuzzy but still sounded good.

Neeka took my earphone and put it over her own ear. Then she got up and did a couple of fancy moves.

"Can't stop this girl," she said, dancing to the music.

She had her back to the street and when I looked over her shoulder, I saw D walking toward us. Only she wasn't alone. There was a tall white woman with her. I stared at her with my mouth hanging open, pointing, with my finger down by my leg, trying to get Neeka's attention.

"Turn around, Neeka!" I said, trying not to move my lips. I waved and D waved.

Neeka turned around then and saw what I saw.

"You think that's somebody from the foster care place?" Neeka said.

The woman had curly light-colored hair and D's same strange green eyes. She was dressed in purple, everything purple—baggy purple pants, too-big purple shirt, black Nikes with a purple stripe. If I'd seen her on the street, I would have thought she was just some freak trying to look fly. But she was with D, so I didn't know *what* to think.

D was smiling, her same old crazy half smile, like she'd just been gone away for a day or a week, not for over a month. But I saw her smile and I felt like my whole body was relaxing, like it had been all tense all the time she was gone and now it could just sit itself down.

We hugged and then we looked at each other and then we hugged again. The whole time, the white lady stood there smiling, like she knew us from way back when or something.

"Ma," D said. "These are my girls." She said our names and the woman's smile got bigger.

"Hey y'all," D said. "This is my moms. We been spending some time together, that's why you ain't seen me around for a while."

Me and Neeka lifted our hands and said something that sounded like *Hi*. We were too busy being shocked that this white woman was D's mama to say anything else.

"Okay," D said slowly. "You can put your eyes back into your heads now."

"Cool to finally meet you both," D's mama said. "Lordy, have I heard some earfuls about you."

She smiled again. Up close she looked like she'd done some hard living. There were lines around her nose and mouth and her skin looked a bit rough. One of her teeth was a little bit crooked, and when she smiled real wide, I could see that one near the back was missing.

"Where you been?" Neeka said, taking off the headphones. "We don't even have your phone number. How you gonna be friends with some sisters all this time and disappear without leaving some digits behind?"

"I didn't know I was gonna turn that corner and not be back for a while," D said. "You know I'm not like that."

She looked up at Neeka's window. Miss Irene had tied some red balloons to her window box.

"Y'all having a party?"

Neeka nodded. "Tash is coming home today. If we'd'a known how to reach you, we would've called."

After a minute she said, "We missed you, D! You can't be leaving your girls hanging like that!"

D looked at me and Neeka. Then she turned to her mama and said, "I'm gonna walk over there and talk to my girls a minute."

D's mama nodded, then checked her watch. "Our bus leaves in two hours, Desiree. We still have to pick up your things."

"Desiree?" I said. "Your name's Desiree?"

Neeka looked on like *Desiree* had grown two new heads.

"That's my birth name," she said. "Desiree Johnson. She's the only one be calling me that."

We walked a little bit away from *Desiree's* mama.

"I thought your last name was Foster," I said.

D shook her head. "Nah, it's really Johnson. I just dropped the Johnson and added Foster because I was in foster care so much."

"We didn't even know your name," I said, more to myself than to D.

"You didn't tell us your mama was white," Neeka whispered.

"I didn't think that mattered," D said. "What difference would it make? You gonna like me less or more because I got a white mama?" She looked at me. "Or because my name wasn't my name?"

"We would have known you some," Neeka said. "That's all. We would have been able to put the D puzzle together a little bit more."

D smiled.

"I came on this street and y'all became my friends. That's the D puzzle. I talked about roaming and y'all listened. I sat down and ate with your mamas and it felt like I was finally belonging somewhere. Us three's the puzzle. It's just a three-piece puzzle."

Neeka shook her head. "You never really told us who you were, girl. We was all the time trying to figure it out."

"But all you had to do was ask."

Neeka put her hands on her hips. "We *did* ask."

"And now the answers are coming," D said. She looked over at her mama. Her voice dropped down a bit. "And anyway," she said, "the D puzzle ain't never going to be all together. I ask her who my daddy is and she says, *A man who likes to roam.* I ask her what it was like when I was a baby and she says, *Alcohol erased that memory, but I don't drink no more.* So the puzzle's always gonna have all these missing pieces, all these *holes* up in it."

Some church ladies moved by us, said hello and headed on up into Neeka's place.

"Y'all know I ain't coming to say good-bye," D said. She was carrying a shoulder bag and she set it down on the curb and reached inside it. "I got something for you." She pulled out a brand-new package of clothesline rope and handed it to Neeka. "The way I figure it, somebody else might come down this block one day and be wanting to be friends with y'all. If she don't have a rope, at least you will."

I felt my eyes starting to get stingy. I wiped them real fast and looked away from D. From *Desiree.*

"Y'all let me play with you once. And when I get upstate, I'm sure there's gonna be some sisters looking for somebody to take the other end of the rope and it's gonna be me all over again. And then I'm gonna get on a bus, head down here and show you how they rocking it up there. But I ain't saying good-bye. I ain't never saying good-bye to you."

"We're Three the Hard Way," Neeka said softly. She was looking down at the rope in her hand, like it was taking her way back to the beginning.

"We always gonna be Three the Hard Way," I said.

Neeka had the earphones draped over her shoulder. She took them off and handed D—*Desiree*—the Walkman.

"It's Tupac," she said. "Keep the whole thing. I know how you love his gangsta behind."

Desiree didn't say anything for a minute. Then she put the Walkman in her bag and threw her arms around Neeka. They stood there, holding each other for a long time. When they pulled away, they were both crying. Then D hugged me.

You're a part of me, she whispered, her mouth close to my ear. *You're in my heart. Forever and always, all right?*

I nodded. If I said one word, I knew I'd start crying and not be able to stop.

"Desiree . . ." D's mama called.

"I'm coming!" D yelled, not turning away from us. "She better cool it or else *I'll* be telling her to step. Be my turn to leave *her*."

Neeka smiled. "You know you're going with that woman. You want a mama too much to let her get away again."

D nodded. She put her hands in her pockets and looked over at her mama. After a moment, she brushed her hair away from her eyes with her hand, squinted into the sun and smiled.

Maybe I'd live to be a hundred. And if I did, I wouldn't

forget that smile. Her green eyes—that were her white mama's green eyes and maybe her mama's mama's green eyes—got bright and sad. When the tears started coming, she didn't wipe them away.

"These two years," she said to me and Neeka. "They was all part of the Big Purpose, you know. We ain't never gonna even try to forget each other. And when we grown and back together again, or when we're all old sitting in rocking chairs somewhere, we gonna remember everything. Every single inch and day and hour and minute and piece of us together now."

"You think we're gonna remember all of it, D?" I asked.

D didn't say anything. Just hugged me and Neeka again and headed back over to her mama. Her mama put her arm around D's shoulder and D grabbed her mama's hand. Only then did she turn around and nod.

"Yeah, girl," she said. "Everything."

Then me and Neeka watched them walk down the street.

"You better call us!" Neeka yelled. "You better write us and stuff."

"You know I will," D yelled back. "Three the Hard Way."

"Three the Hard Way," me and Neeka said back to her. Then Desiree and her mama turned the corner and walked on out of our lives.

CHAPTER TWENTY

Jayjones' first college scholarship offer came from a small school in Maryland. And by the end of the week, letters were coming from everywhere—including Georgetown, where, according to Jayjones, Patrick Ewing had played. I didn't know Patrick Ewing from a can of paint, but Jayjones seemed to think he was something real special because he grabbed Neeka and spun her around their house like he'd lost the very last bit of his mind. Then he picked up Miss Irene and each one of the twins and even Tash. When he went to pick up his daddy, his daddy got there first, picked Jayjones up and spun *him* around. The whole house was dancing around and laughing and making all kinds of noise.

"Start deciding where y'all want to live," Jayjones said. "The way I figure it, in four and half years, we're gonna be moving in!"

Miss Irene invited Mama and some people from church. Tash invited some of his girls from the river and we had a small party that night. Miss Irene had gotten Tash a keyboard as a welcome home present, and when he plugged it in and started moving his fingers over the keys, it was like no time had passed since he was sitting at church making the women dab at their eyes.

Me and Neeka stood beside him.

"Sing 'By and By,'" Tash said.

"Too churchy," Neeka said, turning up her lip.

"You need some 'churchy,'" Tash said, swatting her on the butt. So me and Neeka sang it, and somewhere over the summer, our voices had changed a little bit and grown closer to each other. Her low and my somewhere in between sounded like one voice with a whole lot of different things happening inside it. As we sang, I looked

out at everyone and saw my own mama dabbing at her
eyes.

"By and by, when the morning comes,
You know all saints are bound to come on home . . .
We will tell the story of how we've overcome
and we'll understand it better by and by.
Yes, we'll understand it better by and by . . ."

Neeka's voice went down low and I followed up high. We
looked at each other and smiled as we sang that song, watching to see where we'd take each other. We had a harmony
going, a sad, new familiar harmony that was figuring itself
out. Maybe that was *our* Big Purpose—to figure ourselves
on out.

We got through the first week of school with Miss Irene still taking us and being right there at the end of the day to bring me and Neeka home. I guess since there was other kids getting picked up by their mamas and babysitters and big sisters and brothers and stuff, we didn't look all that strange, but it felt lame. Here we were, already teenagers, and every day, rain, shine or whatever, there was Miss Irene, standing there outside our school.

CHAPTER TWENTY-ONE

"Just keeping you safe," Mama said when I asked her how come me and Neeka couldn't just get home on our own. I'd asked the question a lot over the years and each time we had the same old tired dialogue.

"Safe from what? Ain't nothing out there—" Mama shot me a look. "There isn't anything out there trying to get us, Ma! This is Queens. Nobody trying to mess with nobody from Queens. They too busy messing with people in Brooklyn and Manhattan and the Bronx. Nobody wants to take two trains and a bus to get out here and bother our sorry behinds."

"Because Miss Irene's there waiting for them if they do," Mama said.

I folded my arms. It was Friday evening and Neeka was at church with her family. And D was gone. Wasn't nothing to do but stand and argue with Mama and I wasn't even trying to waste all my breath on that.

"Y'all act like me and Neeka babies."

Mama was standing at the bathroom mirror, plucking her eyebrows. She didn't even blink or turn and look at me.

"Oh, you're acting like a real grown-up right about now, aren't you?" she said. Then went back to plucking.

I turned and headed for the door.

"I'm going to the stairs," I said, letting the door slam hard behind me.

It had rained all day and now the air felt muggy. But the stairs were dry, so I sat down and stared out over the street.

A few doors away, some dads were sitting at a table play-ing dominoes. I could smell their cigar smoke. The dominoes made a hard sound when they hit the table and every once in a while one of the men laughed.

Can't touch that, I heard one of them say.

I saw Tash walking up the street. When he got to the men's table, he stopped and said hi to a few of them. I could see one of them get up and give him a hug. Two of the other men made faces at each other. As he walked away, I heard one of them say, *Glad you home, Tash.* The two men who had made the face leaned in to each other, said something, then laughed. And something about their laughter, the hollow way it echoed down the block, the way Tash tried to walk a little straighter and taller away from it, made me take some small breaths and press my fingernails into my hands to keep from feeling the sadness that filled me up.

"How come you ain't at church?" I said when Tash was close up on me. I wanted to drown out the sound of the laughter behind him, wanted him to forget that men who could laugh at you like that lived so close.

He jumped a little.

"Girl, you trying to scare me half to death. What are you doing sitting out in this darkness by yourself?"

Tash was wearing a light green silky-looking shirt. The top two buttons were open and I could see his skinny chest mus-cles. He'd gotten his hair twisted and the locks were done up in a crown on top of his head. He looked beautiful—not like a beautiful woman. He looked like a beautiful man—like something you wanted to run your hand over and stare at for a long time.

"You looking good, Tash."

Tash rolled his eyes at me. "That doesn't answer my question."

"I'm alone because your mama took my girl to church. How come you ain't there playing the piano?"

Tash waved his hand at me and sat on the bottom step.

"Because it's Friday night and this sister is going out to get her club on! When have you ever known me to step up in church on a Friday night? Shoot. If you see my fingers flying over the keys, the only thing you can be sure of is that it's Sunday!"

I smiled.

"Y'all hear anything from your friend?"

"Nah."

I looked back off down the street. The men were all laughing now and I could see one slap another on the back.

"I know you and Neeka be missing her like crazy."

I shrugged.

"She says she's gonna write us or call when everything settles down. I figure it ain't quite all settled yet."

"As they say up in church—*Well . . . !*"

I smiled. Me and Tash sat real quiet for a few minutes. He looked at his watch, then leaned back on the stair and worked the cuff of his shirt for a bit.

"Tash?"

"Yeah, baby," Tash said, not looking up at me. He'd moved on to the other cuff. When he'd folded them both up just right, he looked at me.

"You ever think about what happened to Randall?"

"No. I know what happened to Mr. Randall. I wouldn't be home if it wasn't for him."

I frowned. "Come again?"

Tash lifted one of his eyebrows and smiled.

"Neeka ain't tell you?"

"Tell me what?"

"Mr. Randall's the reason I got my appeal finally. He got his mind back down in them Georgia hills and let the authorities know it was just some more of that gay-bashing bull that got us all tore up. My stupidity was believing that Sly was trying to get with me. And the stuff that happened at Rikers, they already knew that was self-defense." Tash gave me a fierce look. "I hope you and Neeka ain't trying to mess with any of these wannabe gangstas out here, because it's no good. I'm not trying to be your mama or nothing, I'm just keeping it real."

"Ain't no real gangstas in this neighborhood."

"That's why I said 'wannabe.' Those the worse kind. Try harder than the real ones."

"If Mr. Randall would've died," I said slowly, "you would still be in jail."

"Girl, don't even try to go there. I seen enough jail for two lifetimes."

"You ever see Sly? After that night in Randall's house?"

Tash shook his head. "They weren't trying to put us in the same jail. They knew if they did, only one of us would be walking out alive."

"Which one?" I said. Even though I already knew.

"The one you talking to, Miss Honey. The one you are talk-*ing* to."

Saturday night, Jayjones came running down the street with the news—Tupac got shot again. Four times in the chest by a drive-by in a Cadillac. Critical condition. Some hospital in Las Vegas.

All day Sunday, me and Neeka sat on my bed listening to the radio station, listening to the news.

Surgery.

A lung removed.

We leaned in close to the radio, waiting for more.

CHAPTER TWENTY-TWO

CHAPTER TWENTY-THREE

Early Monday morning, the phone rang. I heard Mama walking slow toward it. I heard her call my name. Then I heard D. I heard Desiree saying real soft and real sad, *Hey girl. Our boy ain't gonna make it.*

And it didn't matter that all those weeks had passed and D had come and gone again. Didn't matter that she'd never told us about her real name or her white mama. It was our girl. It was D. Across all those miles and all that time. It was D up in my ear, all regular, all familiar.

"Girl," I said. "Where the frick-frack you been?"

And then I could feel D smiling.

"It's all complicated with my moms," she said. "But she's trying and I'm trying and I'm up here in these crazy *mountains* with a phone that don't have no long distance! And every day's like a battle just to get through."

I leaned back against the wall in the kitchen and listened to D's voice. I tried to picture her up there in those mountains, wearing a ton of layers and still freezing. Walking the streets with her mama. Roaming.

"Me and Neeka be missing you *crazy*, girl."

"You were supposed to find another person to hold that rope," D said, trying to sound all serious.

I sucked my teeth. "None of these double-handed sisters know how to hold a rope like you."

"I hear that."

"You really think he's gonna die, D."

D got real quiet. Then I heard her say *Yeah,* her voice all shaky and high.

"Me too," I said.

"My moms says people die to make room for other people. She's all up into crystals and afterlife and meditating—that kind of crazy-ass stuff."

I stared out the window. The rain was still coming down and the sky was dark gray and hard-looking. It looked like it was mad at the whole world.

I remembered when my moms said the same thing. I was little then—trying to understand why the two goldfish I'd only had for a week were floating at the top of their bowl. My moms said they'd left this world to make room for other fish. Maybe all mothers learned the same way of talking about dying to their kids.

"You believe her?"

"I guess I do. I hope I do. That would be cool, you know. Then you don't have to be sad—you could just sit around thinking about who's gonna come next. You know if they following Tupac they gotta be bad-ass."

I smiled.

"My moms says you can see where they're going—the people who die. You can meditate and, I don't know, follow them or something."

"That sounds really, really crazy."

D laughed.

"You telling me?! I know my moms is like three fries short of a Happy Meal, but she my moms, so I take what I get."

My mother hollered at me to get off the phone and start getting ready for school.

I told D I had to go.

"You gonna call again? Or you got a number I can call you?"

D gave me the number.

"It works most of the time," she said. "But they be stress-ing you if you don't pay the bill on time and my moms isn't good about that stuff. So if it don't work, just keep trying. She don't let it stay cut off *too* long."

"You called Neeka?"

"Ching-ching. This call is costing me crazy. I got a ten-dollar phone card and I'm sure this call ate it all up! Tell her I thought she'd be at your house where it's quiet."

I laughed. "You better come home soon, D."

A moment passed. And then D said real soft, *You know I will.*

CHAPTER TWENTY-FOUR

On Friday the thirteenth—Tupac died.

In the morning, the sun was out. By noon, the rain started coming down. And just kept on coming.

Me and Neeka sat on the stairs letting ourselves get wet. We must've looked like fools, two girls in rain jackets, our hair all stuck to our heads, ourselves shivering. Maybe we wanted the rain to wash the shock and hurt and confusion away.

Maybe we wanted to go upstairs, dry off and believe Tupac hadn't really died.

When we dialed D's number that night, the phone just rang and rang.

CHAPTER TWENTY-FIVE

Winter came and Jayjones went off to visit
Georgetown. When he came back a few days
later, he was wearing Georgetown everything—
sweatshirt, cap, even his socks said Georgetown.
His grin wide. His basketball spinning on the tip
of his pointer. When the ball stopped spinning,
he looked around—at me and Neeka sitting on
the stairs, wearing the caps he'd brought home
for us.

At Tash, across the street, leaning out Miss Irene's window, a pillow on the sill.

At Neeka's sisters playing hopscotch on the sidewalk.

At Albert, his hands in his pockets, leaning against the stair railing, staring off quietly down the street.

At Emmett, standing near him, trading comic books with his friends.

At my mama, coming down the street, a shopping bag in her hand, saying, *How you doing?* to the people she walked past.

Jayjones held the ball in the crook of his arm. Then he spun it again. Slower, though. And this time, he looked sadder as he watched it turn. Maybe he was already halfway away from all of us. Maybe, inside his own head, he was already shooting baskets and scoring high for Georgetown. Maybe the frown that was between his eyes now was about remembering the summer before and the summer before that when people weren't dying or moving away or losing some big part of themselves.

He bounced the ball once, real hard. Then stuck it back under his arm and headed across the street and on into his house.

"He thinks just because some tired school wants him that he's all that now," Neeka said. "He better remember Tuesday is *still* his day to do dishes!"

I put my arm around Neeka's shoulder and pulled her closer to me.

"You are a true-blue nut, Neeka."

"Yeah," she said. "But I'm your girl anyway."

"True that," I said. "True that."

CHAPTER TWENTY-SIX

It was hard to read anything about Tupac dying and not think about D. Seems D was right—you listen to Tupac's songs and you know he's singing about people like D, about all the kids whose mamas went away, about all the injustice. Brenda throwing away her baby, the cops beating some brother down, the hungry kids, sad kids, kids who got big dreams nobody's listening to. Like over all that time and distance he looked right across the bridge into Queens, New York—right into Desiree's eyes. Strange how he saw her.

He *saw* her.

Some people say Tupac ain't really dead, that he's on some Caribbean island someplace far away from people wanting to shoot him up all the time. And I guess, maybe, I'd do the same thing, I don't know. I mean, how many times can you get shot and get lucky, and be A Miracle like he was?

Jayjones said, "I bet my boy's still somewhere writing songs."

Says he thinks Tupac faked his own death to get away from all that *drama*.

I don't know. Most days I'm still trying to figure it all out. I call D's number and the phone still rings and rings. I check the mailbox and there's never any letter from her. And a part of me gets real sad with the missing of her.

But some mornings, I look out my window and see the sun coming up all crazy orange and gold behind the houses across the street. And sitting there watching it, I have to start smiling. It's hard not to get to hoping that maybe they're together ... finally ... somewhere. Finally meeting each other. Across the miles. Across the years. All the *drama* and *chaos* of their lives dropping away.

D and Tupac. Tupac and D. Walking along some beautiful beach like they be having in the videos. Tupac all dressed in white, his shirt open and blowing in the wind, his beautiful brown chest soaking in all that sun. His sad eyes finally laughing. And D with her hair blowing, her green eyes brighter than anything. Her sweet half smile ... finally whole.

ACKNOWLEDGMENTS

As always, thanks, Nancy, for reading this and rereading this and re-rereading this until it became the story I was trying to tell. Thanks, Sara and Meredith and Charlotte, for all you do. And a big, big thank you to Stephanie Grant—friend and writer extraordinaire—thanks for your amazing eye.

Donald Douglas—thanks for helping me with the basketball stuff. Roman Woodson—thanks for the research.

And all the others who know who they are—Juliet and Patti and Linda and Jill. And the rest of my big and crazy family—for dinner together every Sunday night and the words and phrases and craziness that sometimes make their way to the pages. Thank you. Thank you. Thank you.

And of course, this novel would never have happened without the inspiration that was Tupac Shakur and the many talented musicians that came before, during and after him.

QUESTIONS FOR DISCUSSION

- Explain the characters' varying reactions to the shooting of Tupac Shakur.

- Explain why D is so mesmerized by Tupac in chapter one.

- Explain how, in chapter one, Neeka and the narrator want what D has, and D wants what they have.

- How does the narrator feel connected to D yet jealous of her, too?

- How do Neeka's and the narrator's mothers try to protect them?

- What do you think the narrator means: "Some days D smiled at me and felt like my missing half" (page 43)?

- On page 57, Jayjones says of Tupac, "How come I don't even know him and he be feeling like a brother to me?" What does Tupac seem to mean to Jayjones, D, the narrator and her mother?

- Describe the amphitheater in chapter 11 and explain why the narrator is so moved by being there.

- Describe Tash's experience and how he tries to be strong for the rest of his family. How do we know that Tash is unlikely to have committed the crime he was found guilty of?

- Why, would you say, does the author never name the narrator?

- The narrator says, "Maybe that was *our* Big Purpose—to figure ourselves on out" (page 134). By the end of the story, are any of the characters closer to finding their Big Purpose?

- The rope the girls use for double Dutch is a powerful metaphor for connectedness. Can you identify other forces for connection and wholeness in this block in Queens where Neeka and the narrator live?

- Strong women are important to Woodson's novels. Identify the strong women in *After Tupac & D Foster* and explain what makes them strong.

- Why, do you think, is D Foster the character most affected by the songs of Tupac Shakur, and most affected by the shootings and his death?

- The novel's title is *After Tupac & D Foster;* what do you feel will happen next for Neeka and the narrator? How did D Foster affect them and their way of seeing the world?

- In "If My Homie Calls," Tupac says, "Time goes on, and everybody grows/Grew apart, had to part, went our own ways." Explain how these lines could be the theme of the novel.

Turn the page for a look
at **JACQUELINE WOODSON**'s
moving story of her childhood.

Winner of the National Book Award

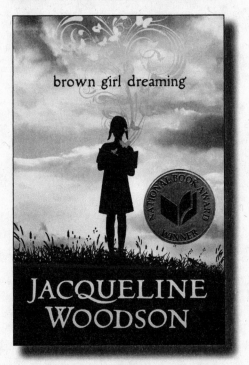

A *Kirkus Reviews* Best Book of 2014

"Gorgeous." —*Vanity Fair*

"This is a book full of poems that cry out to be
learned by heart. These are poems that will, for
years to come, be stored in our bloodstream."
—*The New York Times Book Review*

"Moving and resonant . . . captivating."
—*The Wall Street Journal*

"A radiantly warm memoir." —*The Washington Post*

february 12, 1963

I am born on a Tuesday at University Hospital
Columbus, Ohio,
USA—
a country caught

between Black and White.

I am born not long from the time
or far from the place
where
my great-great-grandparents
worked the deep rich land
unfree
dawn till dusk
unpaid
drank cool water from scooped-out gourds
looked up and followed
the sky's mirrored constellation
to freedom.

I am born as the South explodes,
too many people too many years

enslaved, then emancipated
but not free, the people
who look like me
keep fighting
and marching
and getting killed
so that today—
February 12, 1963
and every day from this moment on,
brown children like me can grow up
free. Can grow up
learning and voting and walking and riding
wherever *we* want.

I am born in Ohio but
the stories of South Carolina already run
like rivers
through my veins.

second daughter's
second day on earth

My birth certificate says: Female Negro
Mother: Mary Anne Irby, 22, Negro
Father: Jack Austin Woodson, 25, Negro

In Birmingham, Alabama, Martin Luther King Jr.
  is planning a march on Washington, where
John F. Kennedy is president.
In Harlem, Malcolm X is standing on a soapbox
  talking about a revolution.

> *Outside the window of University Hospital,*
> *snow is slowly falling. So much already*
> *covers this vast Ohio ground.*

In Montgomery, only seven years have passed
  since Rosa Parks refused
to give up
her seat on a city bus.

> *I am born brown-skinned, black-haired*
> *and wide-eyed.*
> *I am born Negro here and Colored there*

and somewhere else,
the Freedom Singers have linked arms,
their protests rising into song:
Deep in my heart, I do believe
that we shall overcome someday.

and somewhere else, James Baldwin
is writing about injustice, each novel,
each essay, changing the world.

> *I do not yet know who I'll be*
> *what I'll say*
> *how I'll say it . . .*

Not even three years have passed since a brown girl
named Ruby Bridges
walked into an all-white school.
Armed guards surrounded her while hundreds
of white people spat and called her names.

She was six years old.

> *I do not know if I'll be strong like Ruby.*
> *I do not know what the world will look like*
> *when I am finally able to walk, speak, write . . .*
> Another Buckeye!
> *the nurse says to my mother.*
> *Already, I am being named for this place.*

Ohio. The Buckeye State.
My fingers curl into fists, automatically
This is the way, *my mother said,*
of every baby's hand.
I do not know if these hands will become
Malcolm's—raised and fisted
or Martin's—open and asking
or James's—curled around a pen.
I do not know if these hands will be
Rosa's
or Ruby's
gently gloved
and fiercely folded
calmly in a lap,
on a desk,
around a book,
ready
to change the world . . .

a girl named jack

Good enough name for me, my father said
the day I was born.
Don't see why
she can't have it, too.

But the women said no.
My mother first.
Then each aunt, pulling my pink blanket back
patting the crop of thick curls
tugging at my new toes
touching my cheeks.

We won't have a girl named Jack, my mother said.

And my father's sisters whispered,
A boy named Jack was bad enough.
But only so my mother could hear.
Name a girl Jack, my father said,
and she can't help but
grow up strong.
Raise her right, my father said,
and she'll make that name her own.

Name a girl Jack
and people will look at her twice, my father said.

For no good reason but to ask if her parents
were crazy, my mother said.

And back and forth it went until I was Jackie
and my father left the hospital mad.

My mother said to my aunts,
Hand me that pen, wrote
Jacqueline where it asked for a name.
Jacqueline, just in case
someone thought to drop the *ie.*

Jacqueline, just in case
I grew up and wanted something a little bit longer
and further away from
Jack.

the woodsons of ohio

My father's family
can trace their history back
to Thomas Woodson of Chillicothe, said to be
the first son
of Thomas Jefferson and Sally Hemings
some say
this isn't so but . . .

the Woodsons of Ohio know
what the Woodsons coming before them
left behind, in Bibles, in stories,
in history coming down through time

so

ask any Woodson why
you can't go down the Woodson line
without
finding
doctors and lawyers and teachers
athletes and scholars and people in government
they'll say,

We had a head start.
They'll say,
Thomas Woodson expected the best of us.
They'll lean back, lace their fingers
across their chests,
smile a smile that's older than time, say,

Well it all started back before Thomas Jefferson
Woodson of Chillicothe . . .

and they'll begin to tell our long, long story.

the ghosts of the
nelsonville house

The Woodsons are one
of the few Black families in this town, their house
is big and white and sits
on a hill.

Look up
to see them
through the high windows
inside a kitchen filled with the light
of a watery Nelsonville sun. In the parlor
a fireplace burns warmth
into the long Ohio winter.

Keep looking and it's spring again,
the light's gold now, and dancing
across the pine floors.

Once, there were so many children here
running through this house
up and down the stairs, hiding under beds
and in trunks,

sneaking into the kitchen for tiny pieces
of icebox cake, cold fried chicken,
thick slices of their mother's honey ham . . .

Once, my father was a baby here
and then he was a boy . . .

But that was a long time ago.

In the photos my grandfather is taller than everybody
and my grandmother just an inch smaller.

On the walls their children run through fields,
    play in pools,
dance in teen-filled rooms, all of them

grown up and gone now—
but wait!

Look closely:

There's Aunt Alicia, the baby girl,
curls spiraling over her shoulders, her hands
cupped around a bouquet of flowers. Only
four years old in that picture, and already,
a reader.

Beside Alicia another picture, my father, Jack,

the oldest boy.
Eight years old and mad about something
or is it someone
we cannot see?

In another picture, my uncle Woody,
baby boy
laughing and pointing
the Nelsonville house behind him and maybe
his brother at the end of his pointed finger.

My aunt Anne in her nurse's uniform,
my aunt Ada in her university sweater
Buckeye to the bone . . .

The children of Hope and Grace.

Look closely. There I am
in the furrow of Jack's brow,
in the slyness of Alicia's smile,
in the bend of Grace's hand . . .

There I am . . .

Beginning.

it'll be scary
sometimes

My great-great-grandfather on my father's side
was born free in Ohio,

1832.

Built his home and farmed his land,
then dug for coal when the farming
wasn't enough. Fought hard
in the war. His name in stone now
on the Civil War Memorial:

William J. Woodson
United States Colored Troops,
Union, Company B 5th Regt.

A long time dead but living still
among the other soldiers
on that monument in Washington, D.C.

His son was sent to Nelsonville
lived with an aunt

1

His coming into our classroom that morning was the only new thing. Everything else was the same way it'd always been. The snow coming down. Ms. Johnson looking out the window, then after a moment, nodding. The class cheering because she was going to let us go out into the school yard at lunchtime.

It had been that way for days and days.

And then, just before the lunch bell rang, he walked into our classroom.

Stepped through that door white and softly as the snow.

The class got quiet and the boy reached into his pocket and pulled something out. *A note for you, Ms. Johnson,* the boy said. And the way his voice sounded, all new and soft in the room, made most of the class laugh out loud.

But Ms. Johnson gave us a look and the class got quiet.

Now isn't this the strangest thing, I thought, watching the boy.

Just that morning I'd been thinking about the year I'd missed a whole month of school, showing up in late October after everybody had already buddied up. I'd woken up with that thought and, all morning long, hadn't been able to shake it.

The boy was pale and his hair was long—almost to his back. And curly—like my own brother's hair but Mama would *never* let Sean's hair grow that long. I sat at my desk, staring at his hair, wondering what a kid like that was doing in our school—with that long, curly hair and white skin and all.

And he was skinny too. Tall and skinny with white, white hands hanging down below his coat sleeves. Skinny white neck showing above his collar. Brown corduroy bell-bottoms like the ones I was wearing. Not a pair of gloves in sight, just a beat-up dark green book bag that looked like it had a million things in it hanging heavy from his shoulder.

Ms. Johnson said, "Welcome to our sixth-grade classroom," and the boy looked up at her and smiled.

Trevor was sitting in the row in front of me, and when the boy smiled, he coughed but the cough was trying to cover up a word that we weren't allowed to say. Ms. Johnson shot him a look and Trevor just shrugged and tapped his pencil on his desk like he was tapping out a beat in his head. The boy looked at Trevor and Trevor coughed the word again but softer this time. Still, Ms. Johnson heard it.

"You have one more chance, Mr. Trevor," Ms. Johnson said, opening her attendance book and writing something in it with her red pen. Trevor glared at the boy but didn't say the word again. The boy stared back at him—his face pale and calm and quiet. I had never seen such a calm look on a kid. Grown-ups could look that way sometimes, but not the kids I knew. The boy's eyes moved slowly around the classroom but his head stayed still. It felt like he was seeing all of us, taking us in and figuring us out. When his eyes got to me, I made a face, but he just smiled a tiny, calm smile and then his eyes moved on.

I looked down at my notebook. Beneath my name, I had written the date—Wednesday, January 6, 1971. The day before, Ms. Johnson had read us a poem about hope getting inside you and never stopping. I had written that part of the poem down—*Hope is the thing with feathers*—because I had loved the sound of it. Loved the way the words seemed to float across my notebook.

When I told Mama about the poem, she'd said, *Welcome to the seventies, Frannie. Sounds like Ms. Johnson's trying to tell you all something about looking forward instead of back all the time.* I just stared at Mama. The poem was about *hope* and how hope had these feathers on it. It didn't have a single thing to do with looking forward or back or even *sideways*. But then Sean came home and I told him about the poem and the crazy thing Mama had said. Sean smiled and shook his head. *You're a fool,* he signed to me. *The* word *doesn't have feathers. It's a metaphor. Don't you learn anything at Price?*

So maybe the seventies is the thing with feathers. Maybe it was about hope and moving forward and not looking behind you. Some days, I tried to understand all that grown-up stuff. But a lot of it still didn't make any sense to me.

When I looked up from my notebook, Ms. Johnson had assigned the boy a seat close to the front of the room, and when he sat down, I heard him let out a sigh.

Something about the way the new boy sat there, with his shoulders all slumped and his head bent down, made me blink hard. The sadness came on fast. I tried to think of something different, the Christmas that had just passed and the presents I'd gotten. Mama's face when Daddy leaned across the couch to hug her tight. My older brother, Sean, holding up a basketball jersey and signing, *I forgot I told you I wanted this!* His face all broken out into a grin, his hands flying through the air. I put the picture of the sign for *forgot* in my head—four fingers sliding across the forehead like they're wiping away a thought. Sometimes the signs took me to a different thinking place.

The bell rang and Ms. Johnson said, "I'll do a formal introduction after lunch."

All of us got up at the same time and stood in two straight lines, girls on one side, boys on the other. Ms. Johnson led us out of the classroom and down the hall toward the cafeteria. As usual, Rayray acted the fool, doing some crazy dance steps and a quick half-split when Ms. Johnson wasn't looking.

Trevor turned to the boy and whispered, "Don't no palefaces go to this school. You need to get your white butt back across the highway."

"I know I don't hear anyone talking behind me," Ms. Johnson said before the boy could say anything back. But the boy just stared at Trevor as we walked. Even after, when Trevor turned back around, the boy continued looking.

"Face forward, Frannie," Ms. Johnson said. I turned forward.

"You're just as pale as I am . . . my brother," I heard the boy say.

When I turned around again, the boy was looking at Trevor, his face still calm even though the words he'd just spoken were hanging in the air.

Trevor took a deep breath, but before he could turn around again, Ms. Johnson did. She looked at the boy and raised her eyebrows.

"We don't talk while we're on line," she said. "Do we?"

"No, Ms. Johnson," the whole class said.

When Rayray saw how mad Trevor was getting, he looked scared. When he saw me watching him, he pointed to the boy and pulled his finger across his neck.

"If I have to ask you to turn around again, Frannie, I'm pulling you up here with me."

I faced forward again.

Trevor was light, lighter than most of the other kids who went to our school, and blue-eyed. On the first day of school, Rayray made the mistake of asking him if he was part white and Trevor hit him. Hard. After that, nobody asked that question anymore. But I had heard Mama and a neighbor talking about Trevor's daddy, how he was a white man who lived across the highway. And for a while, there were lots of kids at school whispering. But nobody said anything to Trevor. As the months passed and he kept getting in trouble for hitting people, we figured out that he had a mean streak in him—one minute he'd be smiling, the next his blue eyes would get all small and he'd be ramming himself into somebody who'd said the wrong thing or given him the wrong look. Sometimes, he'd just sneak up behind a person and slap the back of their head—for no reason. The whole class was a little bit afraid of him, but Rayray was *a lot* afraid.

As we walked down the hall, I stared at Trevor's back, wondering how long the boy would have to wait before he got his head slapped.